Stranger on Big Hickory

Stranger
on Big Hickory

Stephen W. Meader
Illustrated by Don Lambo

SOUTHERN SKIES

ISBN 978-1-931177-38-2 cloth
ISBN 978-1-931177-39-9 paperback

Library Of Congress Catalog Card Number 64-20975

SOUTHERN SKIES
LITTLE ROCK, ARKANSAS
www.southernskies.com

Dedication

The republication of this book is dedicated with love to Kelly Emmes—avid reader, bright mind, quick wit, luminous woman---by her father who is so proud of her and grateful that she shares her heart with him, Jerry Atchley.

Stranger on Big Hickory

Chapter One

The road ahead was a challenge. Skip stared at the rocks and ruts, the sharp grade that must be climbed, and gripped the wheel harder. If any car in Welbyville could make it, he thought, it was Abigail. He slipped the shift lever into low gear and trod on the accelerator, and the Model-A's tough little engine roared into action. She bumped and swayed and tore through brush, but up she went. At the top of the hill, Skip pulled over on a patch of ferns and looked back proudly at the rugged trail his car had negotiated.

Once it must have been an old wagon track, now long unused, but it had led him to one of the finest views he had ever found. More than a thousand feet below, he could see the little town, stretched along the valley of Blacksnake Creek. There was the square with its bandstand, facing the old brick courthouse. On one corner he could make out the Hickory County National Bank, and on the opposite side was Rollins's Drugstore, his father's place of business.

North Elm Street, where he lived, was nearly hidden by the trees, but the stable roof was visible, and part of his mother's flower garden. It all looked very tiny and peaceful down there in the mid-September morning.

Skip's camera was on the seat beside him, and now he slung the strap over his head and got out of the car to take a picture. The sun, high in the south, was over his right shoulder. He checked the built-in light meter, moved the ring a point or two to the right setting, and sighted through the

viewfinder. It made a nice composition—distant folds of hills, glimpses of meandering river, and the colors of autumn foliage, just beginning to turn. Across the foreground lay the toy buildings of Welbyville. In the sky to the east, there was a momentary glint of sun on metal, and he saw the outline of a jet plane far up in the blue. It was a swept-wing passenger ship, still climbing to make altitude for its dash across the continent.

To the boy, there was nothing strange about the sight, for Big Hickory Mountain lay almost directly under the main flight path from east to west. Yet the country around him was as wild, he knew, as it had been a hundred years before.

When he set out that morning, Skip Rollins had been feeling sorry for himself. It had started the evening before, when he saw Elmer Hunt's station wagon go past. In it, along with Elmer, were three of his schoolmates at Hickory Regional High—Joe Lukens, Dutch Krouse, and a bright-haired girl named Penny Baker. Skip's envy didn't spring from the fact that Penny was riding with the other boys. At least, that was only part of it. He knew they were headed for a meeting of the 4-H Club, and he wasn't a member. Somewhat bitterly, he asked himself why he couldn't have been raised on a farm, like Joe and Elmer. Then he remembered that there were some advantages to being a druggist's son— a chance to dish out sodas at the fountain, for instance, and to get his camera supplies at wholesale. He was popular enough at school, but most of his friends were from out in the country. Penny Baker lived in town, it was true, but she took part in girls' 4-H projects like sewing and making jelly. And the boys were always talking about their calves or pigs or chickens. It was because Skip felt left out that he had decided to invent an activity of his own.

He had his car and his camera, and he liked the woods. Exploring Hickory County would be his private project from now on.

9

Thirty years ago—long before Skip was born—his father had driven the Model-A Ford. He named her Abigail and loved her too much to trade her in. Instead, he put the little car on blocks at the back of the stable, and there she had sat, gathering dust, until Skip got big enough to be interested. Ever since he was twelve, he had tinkered with Abigail. Several times he had taken the engine, transmission, and differential completely apart and put them back together again. The summer before he reached the legal driving age of sixteen, he had earned enough money—mowing lawns, working in the drugstore, and doing odd jobs—to buy a set of used tires, worn, but still with some tread.

Then, on his birthday, his parents had given him the camera. It was a real little beauty—a Retina III-C with such added attachments as an automatic flash and a zoom lens that would bring distant objects amazingly close. It was fast enough, too, to stop almost any kind of motion.

Just as he was turning back toward the car, he saw an animal dart past, crossing the woods road. Skip whipped the camera up, but before he could snap the shutter, the thing was gone. From the single glimpse he had caught, he was sure it was a fox. It had been long and low and rusty-colored, with a big black-tipped bushy tail. Too bad he hadn't been quicker, he thought with regret.

There were more hills ahead, and the woods grew thicker. Up here on the mountain, frost had painted the leaves with bolder hues. The sumacs were crimson along the roadside, and a few birches and hickories were golden in the sun. Skip stopped occasionally to take pictures. But soon the track petered out completely, ending in the dooryard of a long-abandoned farm.

The house itself was gone. All that remained was a brush-grown cellar hole and a forlorn lilac bush beside what must have been the front doorstep. Old, scraggly apple trees grew at the rear, in a clearing now choked with young hemlocks, birches, and sprawling blackberry vines.

The place had such a desolate look that Skip thought it was worth some film. He tried various angles, using the lilac and the gnarled apple branches in his composition. With the camera ready-cocked, he was peering into the viewfinder when a buck deer rose suddenly to its feet in the middle of the orchard. Skip could see the startled ears, the white throat, and the pronged antlers sharply outlined in the frame. He pressed the button in the split second before the buck bounded away.

"Whew!" he said breathlessly. "That was luck! Why couldn't I have been on the ball when I saw the fox?"

He turned the car and drove slowly homeward down the overgrown track. It had been a good morning, but more than that, it had given him the germ of an idea.

How many kinds of wild animals were there in Hickory County, he wondered. Offhand, he might be able to name a dozen that he had seen or heard of, and no doubt there were more. If he counted smaller creatures such as mice and squirrels, he might get as many as fifteen! Would anybody believe it in a place like Welbyville, where folks bragged about living only a hundred miles west of Manhattan?

There was one way to prove it. If he could show actual snapshots or color slides of animals taken within a dozen miles of the courthouse, people would have to admit it was true. Perhaps even the 4-H Club boys and girls would be impressed. If he could make a project out of it, they might take him in as a member!

It was past one o'clock when he reached home. His father had already eaten lunch and gone back to the store, but Skip found soup ready to warm on the stove and sandwiches in the refrigerator. By the time he had his meal out on the kitchen table, his mother appeared.

"Well, Roland," she asked, with a smile, "did you get some good pictures?"

"Yes, Mom," he told her. "But *please*—do you have to call me that? If the other kids heard you, they'd be starting that 'Rollo' stuff again. I got a lot of black eyes making 'em understand my name was Skip."

She laughed. "All right," she agreed. "I guess I was feeling romantic when we christened you, and Roland was the name of a brave, chivalrous knight. But I can see why you'd rather be plain Skip Rollins. Where did you go today?"

He told her about the abandoned farm and the deer. "I can't wait to get this film processed," he said. "I'm positive I

caught him." Then he changed the subject. "What do you think of the 4-H Club, Mom?" he asked.

"From all I've heard, it's a fine organization for young people," she said. "I know Mrs. Douglas, the wife of the County Agent, and she's always talking about the wonderful things the boys and girls do. Why, dear? What makes you ask?"

"Oh, nothing much. I'd sort of like to belong, that's all."

"Well, why not? From what I've heard, a boy doesn't have to live on a farm to take part. Why don't you talk to Cale Douglas? It wouldn't hurt to ask him, anyway."

Skip was pleased at her reaction. That night he wrote down the names of all the wild creatures he could remember having seen, and it made a fairly impressive list. The next day was Sunday. After church he walked to the small, neat house where the Douglas family lived, out on the Indian Rock Road at the edge of town.

Cale Douglas was sitting there on the porch. He was a gray-haired man with a weather-browned face and keen, twinkling gray eyes behind steel-rimmed spectacles. He greeted Skip heartily, asked about his parents, and invited him to sit down.

"Seems as if quite a few of your friends are in 4-H," he remarked. "I've wondered why you didn't join."

"I'd like to, all right," the boy replied, "only I thought it was just for farm kids. I've got an idea, though. Maybe you can tell me whether it would fit in."

Eagerly he began to explain his plan. "I know it wouldn't be easy," he said. "Finding the animals would only be the first part. Then I'd have to get good pictures of 'em—photographs people could recognize. It might take a year or two, and I'd need a lot of luck, besides. But I've got a car and a good camera, and I can find my way 'round in the woods. What do you think?"

The County Agent grinned. "You make me want to try it

14

myself," he said. "Sure—it would come under the heading of conservation—one of our regular projects. Wildlife is a branch of it I don't think anybody else in town has tackled. Come on down to our next meeting, a week from Friday. Meanwhile, go ahead and see what you can do. Here's a pamphlet you might read beforehand."

Skip's step was lighter on the way home. The County Agent's encouragement had been just what he needed, and now he could hardly wait to make a start. Dinner was at three o'clock on Sunday. Over the roast beef he told his father and mother about his plans. John Rollins listened attentively.

"Sounds like a good idea," he said at length. "Just don't get discouraged if it's slow going. You know a deer or a fox isn't going to walk up to you, just asking to be photographed. You'll have to stalk your game like a hunter."

He paused a moment to cut another slice of meat, then appeared to change the subject. "We haven't heard from your Uncle Andy in quite a while, son," he said reflectively. "Guess I'll give him a call tonight."

Skip looked up in time to see his mother give a little smile, and a look of understanding passed between her and her husband. The boy was mystified. He liked Uncle Andy, of course—Andrew Holmes, Mrs. Rollins's younger brother. Andy had settled down now and was doing well in advertising in Philadelphia, but in his younger days he had been something of a rolling stone. He never held a job very long. They might hear from him in Maine one month and in Wyoming the next. When he was hard up for money, he would sell a story to one of the pulp magazines. It wasn't very steady employment, but Skip thought his adventurous life must have been a lot of fun.

When dinner was done, he slung the camera over his shoulder and got into the Ford. There was still plenty of light to take good pictures, and he wanted to finish his roll of color film. Halfway up the side of Big Hickory, he parked the car and ambled off across a stretch of pasture, shooting such scenes as appealed to him as he went. Some sixty feet away he saw a little mound of dirt above the short-cropped grass. Then he heard a sharp whistle, coming from the same direction.

"Groundhog!" he told himself with a grin. "A wild animal? Sure he is!"

Quietly Skip crouched down and sat as still as he could. With one hand he took the zoom lens from his pocket. When it was screwed in place, he waited, hardly breathing, his eyes fixed on the heap of earth. After what seemed like an hour of waiting but was probably no more than two minutes, a gray-brown head popped up out of the burrow. The woodchuck —groundhog, as he was called in Pennsylvania—was a full-grown one, big and fat and wary. After a long look in all directions to make sure the enemy had left, he scrambled out of his hole, ran a few feet, and sat up as tall as possible for another look. Perhaps his keen nose had caught a man scent.

Very slowly Skip raised the camera and spotted the animal in the finder. At the click of the shutter, the groundhog whisked back to safety, but the picture was taken.

Pleased with his first deliberate attempt at wildlife photography, the boy wandered on, down the hill and across a field. High above him he saw a big dark bird gliding on still wings. It was a hawk, he knew, and not a turkey buzzard, for there was no five-fingered spread at the wing tips. Not far from where he stood, there was an old strawstack, and Skip moved toward it, thinking he might hide in its shadow while he watched the winged hunter in the sky. But he was still a dozen steps away when things began to happen.

There was a rustle at the foot of the stack and a tiny, high-pitched squeak. Then he saw a long, slim yellowish body come out of the straw. It was a weasel, carrying a still-struggling field mouse in its teeth. Skip whipped the Retina up.

The zoom lens was still in place, and the distance was about right. In one second he had the picture. In the next, the hawk was swooping down, bullet-fast, to seize the weasel in its talons. The boy had barely time to flip the lever and shoot again. Before he could draw another breath, the big dark bird was flapping powerfully away, its prey squirming in its claws.

Skip sat down on the ground and wiped his forehead. Events had come his way almost faster than he could act. He remembered telling Cale Douglas he would need luck, and he had certainly had his share of it for one afternoon.

After a while he picked himself up and went back to the car, pausing only to remove the zoom lens and check on the number of exposures left in his film. There were only two. He used them up on panoramic shots of the valley and drove home. He could hardly wait to tell his parents what had happened and started talking almost before he was inside the door. When he had poured out some of his excitement, his father chuckled and interrupted him.

"That's fine," he said. "Four-H is a good organization to belong to. I called your Uncle Andy a while ago, and he's coming up here next weekend. Maybe he'll have a surprise for you."

Chapter Two

Monday morning Skip was up extra early. He rushed through breakfast, grabbed his books, and stopped at the drugstore on his way to school. The color film had to be sent off that morning if he wanted slides back by the end of the week. After thinking it over, he had decided to reload with black and white. He knew the Retina would give him good results with the new fast film, and he could do his own developing and printing at home.

One of the first people he saw when he reached school was Penny Baker. It was easy to see where she got her nickname, for the sun flashed on her red-gold hair with the glint of a new-minted copper. At the moment she was talking to another girl, but she turned to greet Skip with a smile

"Hi," he said. "Guess what—I'm going to join 4-H!"

"Really? Why, that's wonderful, Skip. What kind of project are you going to work on?"

He reddened. "It's sort of a new one," he told her. "A kind of conservation thing. Maybe you could call it something like 'The Wildlife of Hickory County.' "

As he said the words, a heavy hand slapped him on the back. Startled, he looked into the grinning face of Dutch Krouse.

"Haw, haw!" the other boy roared. "By golly, that's a project! You goin' to explore the dance hall an' the bar, down to Fink's Roadhouse? If you need any help, just call on me!"

"That's all right, Skip," said Penny comfortingly. "I know what you mean, so don't try to explain to this thick-headed Dutchman. Let him have his joke."

Skip knew Dutch too well to take offense. "I might just want some help, at that," he said with a laugh. "How many kinds of wild animals would you say there are around here, Dutch?"

"That depends on what you mean. If it's things you shoot or trap, I guess maybe seven or eight. How you goin' to prove it?"

"Photographs, mostly. I'll have to spend a lot of time up in the woods, but by spring I hope to show you a bunch of pictures that'll surprise you."

"Huh!" Dutch snorted. "If you can find more'n ten, I'll eat 'em!"

That seemed to be the general opinion among the boys in Skip's group. They were glad he was coming into 4-H but skeptical about his chances of photographing many wild things.

Elmer Hunt summed it up that noon in the cafeteria. "Our farm's right out in the country," he said. "I guess if any critters were around, we'd see 'em. Sure—there's foxes an' coons an' rabbits. Once in a while a deer comes down to the orchard after apples, an' I've heard what sounded like a bobcat screamin', back in the woods. But gettin' close enough for a picture—boy, that's different! More power to you, Skip, but raisin' prize calves is a whole lot easier."

Only Penny seemed to have confidence in his ability to make a go of his project. He told her a little about his first efforts, and she was as eager as he was to see how the slides turned out. On Friday they went to the drugstore together after school, and over double malteds he showed her the transparencies that had come back that day.

The light wasn't very good where they sat. At first Skip

was disappointed, but when he came to the shot of the buck, he felt better.

"Look," he urged, "come on home with me an' I'll rig up the projector. Then we can really tell what I got."

Half an hour later, they knelt side by side in the darkened living room. "All these first ones," he said, as the color came bright on the screen, "are just scenery and stuff. There's your house—see, on the left? And here's our place over here. That's the river, just back of the courthouse roof. Now we're coming to more interesting ones. I found an old farmhouse up on the mountain—just a cellar hole in a clearing. There's the lilac bush by the doorstep. And then, all of a sudden, this deer got up right in front of me."

"Oh!" gasped Penny. "He's beautiful, Skip! Look at those big eyes—it's a wonderful picture!"

When they had admired it sufficiently, he went on to the shot of the groundhog. It was less exciting but clear and sharp, a good example of camera work with the zoom lens. Then he put the slide of the strawstack on the screen.

"What would you say that was, Penny?" he asked.

"Just a pile of straw?"

"No—look there at the bottom in the middle. He's almost the same color as the background. See him?"

"Oh, of course!" she exclaimed. "A yellowish animal—a weasel, isn't it? And he's got a poor little mouse in his mouth!"

"Good for you," said Skip. "Now see what happened about a split second later."

As he replaced the slide, they both sat breathless, staring at the scene that appeared. The shot had been taken just at the instant when the hawk's great talons were about to strike. His fierce yellow eyes, the dark sweep of his wings, the bared teeth of the terrified weasel—all were caught in the picture. By pure luck, Skip had taken a masterpiece.

"Golly!" said Penny shakily. "If I ever had any doubts about your project, they're all gone now. Why, that one day you got four—no, five animals! The field mouse counts, of course, and so does the hawk. What kind was it, Skip? Do you know?"

He nodded. "I looked it up in the bird book. It was a red-tailed hawk—what most farmers call a hen hawk. But birds shouldn't really be included in this project—just wild animals."

It had rained for two days that week, but by Friday night the skies were clear and bright, and there was a hint of coming frost in the air. Just before supper, Skip was crossing the yard when he caught a glimpse of something moving over near the butternut tree. A flash of white stripes on a small brown back told him what it was. The little fellow chirked at him defiantly and made a dash for the tree. "You just stay there," Skip said with a chuckle. "I'll be back in no time."

He raced upstairs and brought down the camera, now loaded with black and white film. There was still good daylight, he thought. Slowly and quietly he moved toward the foot of the butternut, the camera cocked and ready.

"Roland!" came his mother's call. "Supper's on the table!"

At the startling sound, the chipmunk darted down the trunk and for an instant sat looking around with beady little eyes. Skip pressed the shutter button.

"O.K., little buddy," he said with a laugh, "you can relax now and go get some more nuts."

When Mrs. Rollins called again, this time more impatiently, he was able to answer. "Sorry, Mom," he said, as he sat down. "I couldn't holler back that I was coming. Had a date with a chipmunk."

They talked about Uncle Andy's visit. "He might be here tonight," Skip's father remarked. "But it's a good three-hour drive, so I wouldn't blame him if he waited till morning."

"What's that surprise you were talking about?" Skip asked. "You think he's got another new sports car?"

But John Rollins refused to be drawn out. "We'd better just wait and see," was all he would say.

Skip got his homework out of the way for the weekend and went upstairs to bed. Gradually he heard the house quiet down. At eleven-thirty, just as he was falling asleep, there came the throaty purr of an engine in the driveway, and when he ran to the window, he saw a rakish little foreign car below.

"Hi!" he called down. "That you, Uncle Andy?"

"It is, indeed," his uncle replied. "Thought I could sneak in without waking anybody, but I suppose the front door's locked."

Skip dashed down and opened it while Andrew Holmes carried two bags up the steps. One was an old suitcase, fairly large.

"Looks as if you're here for a good long visit," his nephew commented.

"No such luck. I have to go back Sunday, but I brought along something that might interest you. Get yourself upstairs now before you catch cold. The air's a bit sharp tonight."

"Aw, gee! Can't I see it now?"

"Not a chance. Get a good night's sleep, and we'll take a look in the morning. I suppose I'm in the guest room? O.K., I'll find my way."

Despite the fact that it was past midnight before he went to sleep, Skip was up before anyone else the next morning. While he waited for his mother to come down, he set four places at the breakfast table, then went out to get a better look at his uncle's car.

It was new, all right—a gleaming Austin-Healey sportster. He admired the leather-upholstered bucket seats, the wire wheels, the stick-shift on the floor, with its four forward speeds. While he stood there, Uncle Andy himself appeared.

"How do you like her?" the older man asked with a grin.

"Boy—she's a beauty! What'll she do on the road?"

"I don't expect I'll ever find out. At eighty she's just getting nicely warmed up, and that's fast enough for me. Remember, I'm not a wild kid any more. What I like is the smart way she corners on the curves. Hey—I smell coffee! Let's go in."

Skip's mother was a good cook, and having her brother as a guest was cause enough for her to outdo herself. Never had her sizzling ham tasted better, or the eggs, all crinkled around the edges, the fluffy golden popovers, the homemade strawberry jam.

"John," said Uncle Andy solemnly, "I'm not sure you deserve a wife like Myra. If I thought I could find another girl who could cook this way, I'd marry her like a shot!"

When they finally pushed back their chairs, Skip looked at his uncle eagerly. "Now?" he asked.

"Sure, now's the time. Your dad told me you're trying to take photographs of wild animals. Had any luck with it?"

"Just a start," Skip told him. "I'll show you a couple of color slides I thought were pretty good. Wait till I set up the screen."

"Hold it," his uncle put in. "I want to see them, but first let me show you what I brought."

He went to the big suitcase sitting in the hall and opened it. Looking over his shoulder, Skip could see a worn black-leather case inside. Uncle Andy proceeded to take it out and set it on the table, along with something Skip recognized as a folding metal tripod. Next he opened two catches on the black case and lifted the flap. What came into view was a big camera, its leather trim scarred with use but its nickel work gleaming.

"I doubt if you've ever seen one of these before," Uncle Andy said. "It's a Graflex—the kind of camera the big city papers use to get action pictures for a news story. Twenty years ago I had a pal named Ed Willoughby who was a camera bug. We made a lot of trips together, and I'd collect material for nature articles while he took photographs to illustrate 'em. His picture of a big Kodiak bear fishing for salmon in an Alaska river is still famous. But some of his best animal shots were made at night. When Ed died, a few years back, all his equipment came to me, and I can't think of a better use for it than to let you have it."

"Oh, golly!" Skip said slowly. "And I was worrying how I could take night pictures! Has it got a flash?"

"Right in here," his uncle answered, opening a compartment at one end of the case. "You'll have to get fresh batteries and bulbs, I expect, but I think it works as well as ever. Here's where it fits onto the camera. Now we come to the tricky part. See this ordinary little wooden mousetrap? The way Ed worked it, he'd find a path that animals were using and set the trap beside it. If it was a meat-eater he wanted to photograph, he'd bait the trap with bacon or fish. And a strong black thread running back to the camera would trip the shutter and set off the flash as soon as the trap was sprung. For a deer, you wouldn't have to use bait. Just fix another black thread across the path, high enough so the animal's legs'll strike it and spring the trap.

"Your camera, of course, has to be set solidly on the tripod and aimed in the right direction. You get good big pictures, about four by five inches, and the film comes in a flat pack that just loads in the back, here. Why don't you hop in my car and we'll run down to your dad's store? We can buy everything you need there."

Nothing could have pleased Skip more than to settle back in the bucket seat of the Austin-Healey and ride grandly downtown. The only trouble was that on a Saturday morning very few of his friends were around to see him. Older people, such as farmers coming in to market, looked askance at the low-slung little car and didn't appreciate the sporty snarl of its engine.

Uncle Andy never did things by halves. He insisted on paying for two packs of film, batteries, and flash bulbs. The thread, he told Skip with a grin, was no problem. They could liberate a spool of it from Mrs. Rollins's workbasket.

Back at the house, Skip set up the screen and projector and gave his uncle a view of the slides he had taken. The older man was duly impressed.

"I don't have to tell you, though," he remarked, "that opportunities like that aren't likely to come often. I'd call the one of the hawk and the weasel about a once-in-a-lifetime shot. You may have to work harder with the big camera, but I think you'll have a better chance of results."

Skip agreed with him. "I'm crazy to try it out," he said. "Couldn't we rig it up tonight, right here on the place? Dad says something has been eating his late sweet corn, out at the back of the garden."

"O.K.," said his uncle. "But before we make any plans, it seems to me the front lawn could stand a little mowing. Why don't you clean that up while I visit with your mother?"

Skip couldn't argue with that. The fine weather had made the grass grow, and he knew it needed at least one more cutting before frost came. He filled up the mower with gas and got the job done by noon. It wasn't until after lunch that he and Uncle Andy started serious work on the old Graflex.

Chapter Three

The first thing they did that afternoon was take the big camera apart, piece by piece. Skip polished the beautifully ground lens with tissue, getting off the fine dust that had accumulated, careful not to scratch the surface. Each working part was also polished, and a tiny drop of light oil was allowed to soak into the mechanism. They examined the bellows for possible pinholes and found none. After that they put it all together again.

"If I don't get pictures now," said Skip, "it sure won't be the fault of the camera."

Toward sunset they went out through the vegetable garden and looked for a possible animal trail. There were six rows of corn at the back of the lot, four or five hundred feet from the house. It was easy to see where several stalks had been pulled down and the ripe ears removed by sharp teeth.

"Looks like a raccoon's work to me," Uncle Andy commented. "But he doesn't seem to have left any tracks. Probably came down from those woods beyond the fence."

"How would this do?" asked Skip. "Take a nice fresh ear of corn an' drop it out there just beyond the last row. We could set up the camera here, between the stalks, aimed right at the bait, an' rig up the trap an' thread so that if Mr. Coon touches the ear of corn, it'll snap the flash."

"Sounds all right," his uncle replied. "The only way to find out is to try it. You know in the early days of night photography, they used to leave the shutter open in the dark and let the trap set off a pan of flash powder. It's amazing that they ever got good pictures, but some were really remarkable. With this rig, I'd give it a setting of about 1/25 of a second. That ought to stop the motion of a startled animal, and using the flash, I think you may need it that slow. In good daylight, you know, this thing can take pictures even at 1/1000."

"Maybe we ought to see if everything works, first," said Skip. "Let's set it up in the house and give it a test."

They put the camera on its tripod in the front hall, set the mousetrap a dozen feet away, and ran a length of black thread from the spring to the shutter control. Skip extended the bellows to get the proper focus and went back to kneel by the trap. It was then he noticed that the thread was no longer tight. The little wooden base of the trap had moved an inch or two.

"Don't worry about that," his uncle told him. "Out in the field we can fasten it down. Just pull it a bit till the line comes taut and then spring it."

Cautiously the boy moved the trap away from the camera. As he did so, the motion jarred the tiny pan and the spring snapped shut, just missing his finger. At the same instant he was aware of a flash of bright light. It had worked!

"You know what we need?" Uncle Andy suggested. "A size bigger trap. This one's such a hair-trigger little thing I'd be afraid a falling leaf or a raindrop might spring it."

"There's one in the stable," said Skip. "We used to have rats out there. I'll run an' get it."

He found the trap behind an old grain bin, rusty and covered with cobwebs. By the time he got back to the house, he had wiped it off with a rag, and a few drops of oil put it in working order.

"That's better." His uncle nodded. He examined the wooden base carefully. Following his instructions, Skip drilled a hole in it with a brace and bit and drove a large nail through, so that the head was flush with the wood. Pushed into the earth, it would serve to anchor the trap securely.

Before night they had taken the apparatus out to the cornfield and set it up. A fresh bulb was in the flash, the camera was focused on the trap, and the thread, practically invisible in the gathering dark, was drawn tight. Then, very carefully, Skip laid a tempting ear of corn as close to the trigger as he could without touching it off.

"Gosh," he said, "I wish I could sit out here all night an' watch! But that would probably scare the coon off. I'll just have to wait till morning, I guess."

*   *   *

It was always fun to have Uncle Andy around. They spent a pleasant evening listening to his stories of far-off places and talking over old times when he and Mrs. Rollins were youngsters. Skip didn't even think about the camera till he went up to bed at eleven. It was a fine clear night, and the falling temperature gave a warning that frost might come before morning. He couldn't see the corn patch from his window, since it was on the other side of the house. He was sorely tempted to go out and look but decided against it when he thought of getting dressed again. Crawling under the covers, he was soon asleep.

The house was still quiet when he woke Sunday morning, and as soon as he had his clothes on, he tiptoed downstairs. As he had expected, there was a white rime on the grass. With a tingle of excitement, he put on a jacket and hurried out the back door, heading for the corn rows at the rear. As soon as he was close enough to see, he let out a whoop of triumph. The ear of corn was gone and the trap sprung!

A closer examination showed that everything had worked as they planned it. The shutter had been tripped, and there was a burned-out flash bulb in the reflector. Skip collected the equipment and carried it back to the house. He was aching to develop the negative, but those film packs were expensive, and he had six more exposures left in the camera.

His uncle greeted him at the door. "Good morning!" he called. "Did we get a picture?"

"Looks like it," Skip told him. "Anyhow, something set off the flash. Whatever it was that sprung the trap must have had quite a scare when the light went off, but he wasn't too frightened to carry away the bait!"

"Did you find any tracks?"

"Gee, I forgot to look! The ground was pretty dry, though, an' I doubt if he left any."

Uncle Andy had to start back shortly after noon that day, but there was time for them to discuss more picture possibilities.

"You may be surprised," the older man said, "when you find out how much goes on in the woods at night. A lot of animals don't stir out in the daytime, but as soon as it's dark, they prowl around looking for food. The main thing is to find their trails and set up your camera there."

"I know," Skip agreed. "There's some real wilderness over back of the mountain—rock ledges an' caves an' swampy streams. That's where I plan to try next. Wish you were staying a week or so, Uncle Andy. We could have some fun!"

After he had waved good-by to the sports car, he packed the big camera and the rest of the equipment into the old Ford, took along the Retina for luck, and drove up over the shoulder of Big Hickory. He remembered seeing a narrow little track that led northeastward into the woods, and now he meant to explore it. When he came to the place, it was so well hidden by brush that he drove right by. Only when he had gone on a quarter of a mile was he sure he must have passed it. Turning around in that narrow road was difficult, but he finally made it and drove back very slowly.

The gap where the trail led in was barely visible. Apparently no car had ever used it. Skip got out, pulled away some fallen limbs, and cut back some brush with his jackknife. There was a trail there, all right—probably made by lumbermen's sleds years before. He measured the width with his eye and decided against asking his precious Abigail to navigate it.

Pulling over to the side so that he wouldn't completely block the road, he took his small camera and started up the woods trail on foot. After a few minutes he found the rough ground sloping away to the left. Eastward, on his right, the woods ran upward toward the mountain's summit. The brush grew thicker, forcing him to crouch and plow forward along the trail with both hands shielding his face. He was coming to a swampy place now. His feet squelched in hidden water that lay under the leaves.

Stopping, he tried to peer under the bushes in front of him. Unless he was mistaken, the ground appeared to be a little higher beyond, so he pushed on once more, stepping on the roots and tufts of grass that stood above the water.

Suddenly he heard a splashing sound ahead. He waited, holding his breath, and after perhaps half a minute it came again. Stare as he would, he could make out nothing moving in the swamp, but the next time he heard the noise, he was sure it was at a distance. It sounded like a big fish jumping in a lake.

His curiosity was strong now. Advancing as quietly as possible, he soon found himself on a ridge of dry ground among some fairly large trees. And between their trunks he could catch a glint of water. Cautiously he moved on a few steps, readying the camera as he went. There, below him, was a pretty little stream, not over twenty feet across, flowing gently toward the south.

He was still looking at it in surprise when the sound of a splash came again, this time from up the stream to his right. Stooping for a better view, he saw a dark, sleek head moving rapidly up the creek, with a V of ripples behind it. His heart jumped. The creature was far too big for a muskrat—it must be an otter!

His guess was confirmed a moment later when the animal slipped out of the water, gave itself a quick shake, and glided up the steep bank. The glistening brown body and thick, tapered tail were unmistakable. It was surprisingly large, too —at least the size of a cocker spaniel, but longer and shorter-furred. With hands that trembled, Skip pulled the film lever and adjusted the light setting. Whether the otter had seen him or not, he wanted to be ready for a shot if the chance offered.

The long, slim animal was still visible in the brush at the top of the bank. It moved around a small huckleberry bush and reappeared at the head of a smooth strip of clay that ran down into the stream. Skip got his eye to the finder just in time. As he clicked the shutter, the otter dove head first down the slide and went in with a splash exactly like those the boy had heard before.

Quickly he took another picture of the playful creature swimming back to shore, and since it seemed to be unafraid of his presence, he continued to make action shots of one slide after another, enjoying the fun almost as much as the otter.

At last his subject grew tired of the game, dove under the surface, and darted away downstream so fast that Skip couldn't follow its progress. He got to his feet and started back toward the road, still in a kind of daze. This time he kept more to his left, to avoid the swamp, and made his way along the hillside. It was on the higher ground, less than a hundred yards from the car, that he stumbled across a deer path.

There were tracks in the soft earth—made by a doe and her fawn, he thought. And numerous droppings made him sure the path was regularly used. It seemed like an ideal place to set up the Graflex. He looked at his wrist watch, saw

there would still be time before he was expected home, and hurried down to the parked Ford. In twenty minutes of hard work, he carried the equipment back to the deer trail, set up the tripod and camera, and stretched a thread about fifteen inches above the ground. One end was run over a sapling limb, then down to the delicately set rattrap. The other he attached to a bush. Then he stretched a second length of thread from the trap to the camera. Any animal bigger than a fox that came down the path in the night would get its picture taken.

Finally satisfied, he started back toward the car. He had taken less than a dozen steps when he heard the faint snap of a twig that seemed to come from somewhere on his left, up

the mountainside. Skip waited and listened. The stillness that hung over the woods wasn't broken again except for the scolding of a blue jay. Probably, he concluded, the noise he had heard was made by some small animal. It could even have been an acorn dropped by a squirrel. Anyhow, his watch told him he would have to hurry to be home in time for dinner.

The drive down into the village was soon accomplished, and he pulled into the yard just as his mother was putting the roast on the table. All through the meal, Skip could talk of nothing but the otter he had seen at play.

"I must have taken eight or ten shots," he told his parents. "There ought to be some good ones out of that many. I was wishing I had a movie camera, but the whirring noise would probably have scared him off."

After dinner he went over to Penny's house, eager to tell her about his experience. Unfortunately, he found she had gone for a ride with her parents, so he wandered on home. Along the way, a small worry began to gnaw at his mind. Was he sure about that noise he had heard in the woods? The camera was valuable and might prove pretty tempting to boys who came across it. Perhaps they had even been watching him!

Quickening his stride to a run, he got out the old Ford and went charging back up the mountain. Everything seemed peaceful enough over on the south slope. He encountered no humans, young or old, and the only tracks leading in from the roadside were his own. Hurriedly he clambered up the hill from the woods trail till he reached the deer path and heaved a sigh of relief when he caught sight of the Graflex on its tripod. Then something else came into view. It was the trap, pulled up and tossed into the brush beside the camera. Both threads had been broken, yet the flash bulb in the reflector was still unfired.

Skip's puzzlement gave way to a slow anger. No four-footed beast had done this. He looked over the ground carefully and found what looked like a man's track. It wasn't one of his own, for there was no heel print, and he thought it must have been made either by a moccasin or a smooth-worn sneaker.

The discovery was dismaying, to say the least. Somebody must be bent on stopping his animal photography. A thief would have taken the camera, and a vandal would have smashed it. What this man had done was merely give him warning to stay out of the woods, but why he couldn't imagine.

Skip hesitated a moment, then reluctantly packed up the gear and carried it back to the car. Somehow he would have to find another way.

Chapter Four

On Monday he talked to Penny at school and poured out his frustration. "I've been wondering," he said, "if it could be just a trick pulled by one of the boys. You know how they laughed at the idea of my project. Think Dutch or Joe or Elmer would do something like that?"

"No," she told him firmly. "I don't think there's anything really mean about any of them, and if they'd wanted to try a practical joke, they'd have seen to it that you got a picture— of a dog or a pig or something. Anyhow, I'm sure they'd have been so full of it, one of them would tell me."

"That's what I figured." Skip nodded. "But if they didn't do it, who do you suppose did? Here I've got a perfectly swell camera for taking night shots an' don't dare use it!"

Penny chuckled. "I guess you'll just have to wrap up in a blanket and stay there to watch it all night," she said. "But you've still got the small camera for daytime pictures. Did you take any more?"

He told her about the otter slide, and Penny immediately wanted to go and see it, too.

"All right," he said. "I'll take you tomorrow afternoon if you can get away. I have to work in the store today. It shouldn't take more'n an hour to get up there—but wear old clothes an' shoes. There are wet spots over back of the mountain."

School was out at three on Tuesday, and by four o'clock Skip and Penny were driving up the Big Hickory road. They left the car and went into the woods on foot, following the trail till they reached the swamp. There they made a detour up the hillside and finally came down again to the spot where Skip had watched the otter.

This time they heard no happy splashing. The stream ran still and dark under the overhanging trees. Disappointed, they waited for a while, hoping the animal would appear, but after ten minutes Skip give up.

"Let's go on a little way upstream," he whispered. "Could be he's got a den in the bank somewhere along here."

Soon they were opposite the clay slide where Skip had seen the otter disporting itself. He pointed it out to Penny, but she was looking at something a few feet beyond.

"See that hole?" she said. "Right down by the edge of the water. I thought I saw something move there a second ago."

He looked where she pointed. The hole was perhaps eight inches in diameter and seemed to run under a root, straight into the bank. Then he noticed something else. Wedged across the opening, with one end caught on the root, was a three-foot stick of wood that looked as if it had been cut with an ax. And fastened around its middle was a thin chain!

"That's the clog on a trap!" Skip exclaimed. "Whatever's caught in it must be inside the hole, and I bet it's the otter!"

Penny's face was pale. "Oh, the poor thing!" she murmured. "We've got to get over there and let it out."

The water was deep and cold where they stood, but some fifty yards up the stream, they could see a fallen tree that extended most of the way across. Together they hurried toward it, climbed up through the maze of roots, and reached the trunk.

"I'll go first," said Skip, "an' see if it's safe."

He felt the tree spring disconcertingly under his feet but went on, balancing with his arms. At the farther end he had to hold onto a branch and swing out across the last few feet of water. When he was safely on the farther bank, he turned to warn Penny not to try it. But she was already almost over, running lightly along the log. She seized the branch and jumped, and he caught her arm, pulling her up beside him.

"Quick!" she said. "I can't wait to help that animal get free!"

"Wait a second, Penny," Skip answered. "Here's a track in the soft ground. A man's shoe, I'd say, an' pretty good-sized."

She nodded. "Is it anything like the one you found near the camera? Well, no wonder he wants to keep you out of the woods, if he's trapping here against the law!"

Skip hesitated. "It could be the same man," he said, "but if so, he's changed his shoes. This one's got a heel."

They scrambled on through the brush till they were just above the den in the bank. The clog moved a little, as if something inside had pulled on it.

"I don't know if I can get him out," Skip said, "but I've got to try."

He soon found there was only one way. Without waiting to take off his shoes and roll up his trousers, he got down into the water, perhaps two feet deep there by the bank, and took a firm hold on the clog. The animal resisted his tugging with all its strength, but little by little Skip pulled the chain toward him.

"Keep on!" Penny urged. "He's almost out. I can see the trap now."

With a final violent heave, the boy jerked the trap and the otter free and toppled backward into the stream. He hung onto the clog, however. In another moment he scrambled, dripping, up the bank. Penny was doing her best not to laugh.

"Here," Skip panted. "Keep hold of this while I get my jacket off."

Obediently Penny clung to the chain. The frantic animal thrashed about, trying to pull out of the cruel jaws that held its hind foot, but it made no effort to attack her.

"Now," said Skip, "I'm going to open the trap, but you'll have to hold him down under this windbreaker."

He flung the stout leather jacket over the otter's head and body and pressed down on the trap's spring with his knee. The jaws parted, and the animal pulled its bleeding leg clear. Even before Penny could lift the jacket, it had squirmed free and made a dive for the creek. They had one glimpse of the sleek brown body darting off under water, and then it disappeared.

"Well," said Penny with a grin, "you got pretty wet, but you've done your good deed for the day! What'll we do with this miserable thing?" She touched the trap with her toe.

"I've got to be fair," Skip told her. "The guy who set it—if it *was* the same guy—didn't smash my camera or steal it. So I aim to leave his trap right here. We've made so many tracks he'll know who let the otter out, but now we're even. Come on—let's go home. My clothes are so wet I may as well wade and carry you across."

Penny was still worried about the injured otter as they drove home. "How bad did his leg look to you?" she asked. "Do you think he'll get well, or will he lose a foot?"

"I couldn't really tell," Skip answered. "He'd pulled on it so hard, the flesh and sinews were pretty much chewed up, but I don't think any bones were broken. I sure hope he makes it. Animals are supposed to have an instinct about damage like that and know how to take care of themselves."

*   *   *

It rained for two days that week, but Skip managed to finish off the film in the smaller camera. He had his own darkroom in the basement and had learned to do a fair job of developing and printing. More than that, if a picture seemed to be worth enlarging, he had the apparatus to do it.

Each evening he hurried through his homework and went down to the cellar. Out of the twenty frames in his 35-millimeter film, only nine were pictures he could use in his project. The first one was the shot he had taken of the chipmunk, and though the light hadn't been perfect, it was clear and recognizable.

When he came to the strip of otter film, however, he grew excited. The eight shots showed the graceful animal in a variety of positions—climbing the bank, poised at the top of the slide, coasting down with a splash, and swimming back to shore. He decided that all of them were worthy of blowups. Carefully he adjusted the light and timing and set to work. By Thursday night he had a series of eight-by-ten enlargements that any photographer might be proud of.

On Friday he saw Penny again and asked her where the 4-H Club meeting was to be held.

"It's at the Grange Hall tonight," she told him. "Usually we meet around at members' homes, but this is the monthly session when we report on our projects. You be sure to come, now, and bring your Kodachromes. Are the otter pictures finished, too?"

Skip nodded. "You'll be surprised," he said. "They all came out fine. See you tonight."

He packed the screen and projector in the car after supper, took his carefully wrapped slides and blowups, and set off for the Grange Hall. He was one of the first to arrive. Cale Douglas, the County Agent, was there, and a younger man named Ed Jones, who was the club leader.

Douglas introduced Skip. "Ed'll show you what you've got to learn if you're to be a full-fledged member of 4-H," he said. "I see you've brought some pictures. We'll all be glad to have a look at them."

Skip studied the pamphlets Jones gave him while he waited for the others. They outlined the purposes of 4-H and the standards the organization demanded of its members. "Head, Heart, Hands, and Health"—the meaning of each was made clear. By the time the fifteen boys and girls were assembled, Skip had learned the pledge and knew he could repeat it:

> "I pledge . . .
> my HEAD to clearer thinking,
> my HEART to greater loyalty,
> my HANDS to larger service, and
> my HEALTH to better living, for
> my club, my community, and
> my country."

Soon he was saying it with the others and feeling the solemn meaning of the words. It was Elmer Hunt who had called the meeting to order. Now he consulted the notes before him.

"First order of business," he announced, "is to act on an application for membership. Seems one of our neighbors and schoolmates would like to join 4-H. Fellow signs himself"— he pretended to have difficulty in reading the name—"Roland H. Rollins. Anybody ever hear of him?"

There was a roar of laughter from the boys and titters from the girls.

"O.K., Skip," Elmer said with a chuckle. "Before we vote on you, we have to hear what kind of project you aim to tackle."

"Conservation," Skip replied with a straight face. "Forestry and Wildlife. Project Number Four. Wild Animals."

Only Dutch Krouse laughed when he made this statement, and the big fellow quieted down after Elmer pounded the table with his gavel.

"That's an approved project," the presiding officer commented. "So the application seems to be all in order. Ready for the motion?"

"I move he be accepted," Penny called out, and Joe Lukens seconded the motion. A minute later Skip found himself a member of 4-H.

The meeting continued in a businesslike manner. One by one the members got up and gave progress reports on their special projects. Penny and three of the other girls were working on pinafores for the little girls at the orphanage up the valley. So far they had made twenty of them and showed samples of their handiwork.

Dutch Krouse was raising a hog he planned to show next month at the Hickory County Fair and was proud of the fact it now weighed more than four hundred pounds. Several of the boys lived on dairy farms and were raising their own calves, with a considerable amount of good-natured rivalry. Elmer Hunt's pure-bred Guernsey heifer appeared certain to take some kind of ribbon at the fair.

There were other projects that concerned chickens, sheep, and horses. But one of the most interesting to Skip was the work Joe Lukens was doing with bees. He had nine hives now, he told them, and expected to market close to five hundred pounds of prime clover honey.

"The crop's about all made now," he explained. "Not much bee feed left but goldenrod. Tomorrow I'll be taking the honey out of the hives. This year I've got an extractor, so I can sell it in jars. If anybody wants to come up an' watch, they'll be welcome."

"Not me!" said Dutch. "I got stung by some of your bees last fall."

"I'd like to see it," Skip said, "but I can't promise to stay very long. I'm going up on the mountain tomorrow."

When all the rest had given their reports and demonstrations, Dutch Krouse moved the business meeting be adjourned. "Come on," he proposed. "Let's have some eats an' some fun!"

"Wait!" Penny Baker put in. "What about Skip? He's already started his project, and he's got pictures to show us."

Dutch's motion was voted down. He lolled back and grumbled while the screen was being set up.

"This is just a beginning," Skip apologized. "The project outline says the animals have to be seen and identified and a study made of their habits. So far all I've done is get a few pictures that prove I've seen 'em."

Without further comment he asked that the lights be turned out and threw a color slide on the screen.

"This is a big old groundhog I got a shot of, up on the hill," he said. "His Latin name is *Marmota monax*. Most places he's called a woodchuck, and that comes from an Indian word—*wejack*."

He put on the next slide. "Anybody recognize this one?" he asked.

"Looks like a weasel," Elmer Hunt offered. "Got something in his mouth, too—a mouse."

"Right. It's a field mouse he'd caught in that strawstack. The weasel belongs to the genus *Mustela*. Now see what happened to him about two shakes later."

The picture of the hawk pouncing on its prey brought gasps from the boys and excited squeals from the girls.

"Gee!" said Joe Lukens admiringly. "You really can handle that camera!"

"Not really," Skip answered. "I was just awful lucky. And it was the same way with this one. I thought I was taking a shot of an old cellar hole when up jumped a buck deer!"

The black and white prints he showed them after the lights came on again were something of an anticlimax. However, the pictures of the otter at play came out strong and clear, and his audience responded with plenty of interest.

"So," he concluded, "if you count the chipmunk and the field mouse, I've made a fair start—five animals. Next month I hope I can show you some more."

The applause was genuine. Even Dutch grudgingly admitted that he had a pretty good project. "Reckon you ain't likely to get many more, though," he added.

When the meeting was over, they square-danced and ate

ice cream and cookies prepared by the girls. At eleven the good nights were said. Skip took Penny home in his car.

"How do you like 4-H?" she asked, and he needed little time to answer.

"It's swell!" he told her. "I wish now I'd joined up long ago."

Chapter Five

Joe Lukens lived on a two-hundred-acre farm north of town. His father raised apples and had a few dairy cows as well. It was partly because of the apple orchards that Joe had gone in for bee-keeping, knowing bees were needed to pollinize the blossoms in the spring.

Skip drove up to the farmhouse about ten o'clock that Saturday morning. Mrs. Lukens greeted him at the kitchen door and told him Joe and his father were over in the west field, where the hives were located. With his small camera slung over his shoulder, he set off up the lane to find them.

He was still some distance away when he spotted the figures of Joe and Mr. Lukens silhouetted against the dark woods at the mountain's foot. Skip skirted the orchard and cut across the field. As he came closer, he saw Joe standing dejectedly at one end of the row of hives. In front of him was what looked like the wreckage of a broken box.

"Hi, Joe," Skip hailed him. "What's the trouble?"

"Plenty!" the other boy growled. "Some durn varmint busted into a hive an' stole about fifty pounds o' honey!"

"Gosh!" said Skip. "What kind of an animal was it—do you know?"

"How can I tell? Coon, maybe, or a fox. We just got here a few minutes ago."

"Well," Skip told him, "I'm going to look for tracks. Want to come along?"

Back at the edge of the field, there was a low spot near the

woods. It was damp from the frost and muddy. And there, as plain as if it had been left for a signature, was the print of a bear's hind foot.

"We might have known," said Joe's father gruffly. "Never was a bear that didn't love honey. Only I wouldn't have believed we'd had any bears in these parts for years. We'd better get your honey out o' the hives right now an' decide where to move 'em. That old cuss is sure to come back for more."

Skip was measuring the track with a stick. "He's a pretty good-sized bear," he commented. "Full grown, wouldn't you say, Mr. Lukens?"

"Yep. That track must be nine or ten inches long. A bear that big, fattening up before winter, might like a good plump calf, too. I'd better go call the game warden an' see if we can get rid of him."

He got in the pick-up truck and drove back to the house, while Joe started taking the supers off the hives. Each one held twenty-eight blocks of well-filled honeycomb, weighing nearly a pound apiece. The worker bees, flying back to the hive, seemed surprised to find the frames gone, but they buzzed around aimlessly and made no attempt to sting the boys.

When Mr. Lukens returned with the truck, they loaded the honey aboard, then stood talking about a safer place to put the hives.

"Could I ask you one favor, Joe?" Skip put in. "If you could leave that one the bear knocked apart, I bet he'll be back tonight. I've got a flash camera I'd like to rig up an' try to catch a picture of him."

Joe agreed at once, but his father was somewhat doubtful. "The warden plans to come up here with dogs an' trail the critter," he said. "It's out o' season, but he's allowed to shoot a bear that's damaging property. Said he'd try to get here this afternoon."

On the chance that the game warden wouldn't show up, Skip drove home and got the Graflex. For that day, at least, he had decided the Lukens' farm offered more chance for excitement than a trip to the mountain. As an afterthought, he also brought along a panful of dry plaster of Paris. One of the rules laid down in his 4-H project was that if a photograph couldn't be obtained, a plaster cast of a footprint would serve as identification.

The track at the edge of the woods was still undisturbed when he returned. He mixed the plaster with water, covered the print with a thick layer of it, and waited for it to set. Joe was more interested in the camera and trap. He helped Skip place the tripod a few yards from the broken hive. Then they set the rattrap and put it in a puddle of spilled honey close to the hive, running a thread back to the camera shutter.

By that time the cast had dried. Skip lifted it carefully and found it had turned out even better than he hoped. Every toe mark was clear, even to the deep, sharp prints of the claws.

"Company coming!" Joe announced. "That must be Tom Blake, the warden. I can see dogs in the back of the station wagon."

The car drove up the lane and across the field. Mr. Lukens was in the front seat with the state officer. As soon as they dropped the tail gate, a pair of big, rangy hounds jumped down.

"Gosh!" said Skip. "I'd better pick up that trap before they start hunting for a scent, or they'll set off the camera!"

He was barely in time. The dogs went at once to the broken hive, nosed around it, and then one of them lifted his head to whimper with excitement.

"Good boy, Ranger!" called the warden encouragingly. "Let's see you follow him now!"

He had taken a repeating rifle from the station wagon, and as the hounds moved off toward the woods, he followed. Skip hurried after him, clutching the small camera.

"Mr. Blake," he asked, "could I come along an' maybe take a picture?"

But the warden shook his head. "I've got to handle this alone," he replied. "Don't want anybody getting shot or clawed. You folks'll have to stay back here."

Disappointed as he was, Skip had to admit the order made sense. He waited till the bugle notes of the hounds had faded out in the woods high on the mountainside. Then he went to help Joe with his honey.

The extractor was big enough to take two frames at a time and was hand-operated. As Skip turned the crank, he could see a golden stream of the sweet, sticky liquid flowing into the stainless steel milk pail placed under the spout. When a pail was full, it was carried into the shed, where a lot of empty new pint jars stood in rows. After the honey had been strained, it had to be poured into the jars and tightly sealed.

"I dunno," said Joe, eying the last two frames. "This looks so pretty in the comb boxes, I think I'll try to sell it that way. I bet some folks still like it better right in the comb."

"Where do you aim to sell it?" Skip asked.

"Different markets. Johnson's Cash-an'-Carry said they could handle two hundred pints o' fall honey. I already sold 'em more'n that back in July. That was clover honey, though, an' this is part goldenrod. It's got a little different taste an' it's darker, but just as good. Here—try a slice o' comb."

He cut off a generous slab with his knife and handed it to Skip. One taste made him want more. In three minutes he had finished the delicious stuff and was wiping his hands on the grass.

"Man!" he told his friend. "I've got to take some of this home to my folks. How much do you get for it?"

Joe laughed. "No charge to you. Take the rest of this block. I'll wrap it up tight, so it won't drip."

Once the honey was ready for market, the next job was to move the hives to the orchard, nearer the house. Joe banked leaves and sawdust around them, leaving an entrance hole clear, and checked each one to make sure there was enough old honey to feed the colony through the winter.

"They don't eat much when they aren't working," he explained. "After cold weather comes, they go to sleep in the hive an' only a few come out on sunny days. I'll put these frames close by, so they can clean 'em out an' store the honey in the hives. In a couple of days, the supers'll be cleaner'n you could get 'em with soap an' water."

It was late afternoon when the job was finished, and there was a sharp nip of frost in the still air. From time to time Skip had cast an envious eye toward the woods, wondering how the bear hunt was progressing. Now, as the October dusk settled, he heard an engine start, up in the west field. The game warden was returning in the station wagon with his dogs.

"Any luck?" Joe's father asked him when he drove up.

"Nope," he replied grumpily. "Lost the trail on the bare ledges, up near the top. The hounds cast around for better'n an hour but never could pick it up again. Anyhow, I see you've got the hives moved, an' I reckon the critter's had enough of a scare so he won't come back. Let me know if you have any more trouble."

With that, he let in the clutch and drove away.

"I've got to get home to supper," said Skip. "But first I want to reset that trap that works the Graflex, just in case the bear does come back."

Joe went with him, and it took them only a few minutes to

replace the trap and thread. "Aren't you scared he'll smash your camera?" the farm boy asked.

"Have to take a chance on that if I want a picture. Anyhow, I reckon the flash would scare him so he'd run clear out of the county!"

*　　*　　*

It was barely daylight Sunday morning when Skip was wakened out of a sound sleep. Dimly he became aware that the telephone was ringing downstairs. Then it stopped, and he heard his father's sleepy voice answering.

"Somebody wants a prescription filled an' can't wait till after breakfast," Skip thought drowsily. He snuggled back into his warm nest under the covers and closed his eyes.

"Skip!" his father called. "Get up—you're wanted on the phone."

Skip groaned but obeyed. He got into slippers and bathrobe, shut the window, and went downstairs. An excited voice answered when he spoke into the phone.

"Hey! The bear did come back!" Joe Lukens told him. "The camera's O.K., but the trap's sprung an' the flash bulb's burned. I went up there before I did the chores an' found where he'd stepped in that spilled honey. Same big tracks!"

"Gee, thanks, Joe!" Skip answered, thoroughly awake now. "I'll come up there just as soon as I'm dressed!"

He didn't wait for breakfast but drove to the Lukens' farm as fast as Abigail could travel. Joe was waiting for him at the house, and together they drove to the west field. There was no question that the bear had been back. The broken hive box was mashed flat, and there were tracks all around the spot.

"I wonder what Mr. Blake would say to this," Skip told his friend with a grin. "He seemed pretty sure he'd scared the bear off."

"I'm afraid it's nothing to laugh about," said Joe. "You heard what Dad said about his calves. Usually we let the young stock run, up in the back pasture, till snow comes. Now I reckon we'll have to keep 'em in the barn at night."

"You're right, and I'm sorry," Skip said. "Anyhow, it looks as if I'd got the old cuss's portrait. There are some more films in the pack, but I can't wait to develop this one and another I took. So stand by while I shoot the rest. You don't mind posing for a picture or two, do you?"

He reset the shutter for daylight and took action shots of Joe doing his chores around the barn. Then he hurried home, arriving just as his father and mother were sitting down to breakfast. By the time he had to start for church, he had put his film in the developer.

There were two negatives he particularly wanted to see, and he took a look as soon as he got back. The first one he came to was a surprise. He had fully expected a shot of a black-masked raccoon among the cornstalks. Instead he saw a slightly smaller animal, gray-furred, with a long snout and a smooth tail like a rat's. Skip had never seen a live opossum, but he was sure that was what it was. Looking more closely, he could make out a handlike paw turning the ear of corn he had used as bait. That action must have sprung the trap and fired the flash.

To make certain of the species he had caught on the negative, he went to the big dictionary in his father's study. Sure enough, there was the 'possum—beady eyes and small ears, plump gray body and curling, hairless tail.

Next he found the negative taken the night before. It would be better when the print was made, but even in its present state, the bulk of the bear was easily recognizable, as was the great fore paw, lifted to smash again at the hive.

That afternoon Skip printed his pictures, and both the

animal films came out splendidly. He showed them to his parents with pride.

"I bet you didn't know it was a 'possum that was stealing your corn," he told his father.

"No," said John Rollins. "I was pretty sure it was a coon. I had no idea there were any opossums this far north. They must be pretty rare, at that."

Early in the evening, Skip took the two pictures over to Penny's house. A lot had happened in the two days since he saw her at the 4-H meeting, and he was very proud of the results he had gotten with the Graflex. While she was exclaiming over the prints, the phone rang. It was Joe Lukens, asking for Skip, and he sounded excited.

"Guess what!" he said. "Tom Blake went after the bear again today, an' I heard a couple of rifle shots up on the mountain! That was about five o'clock. He isn't back yet, but I bet it's because he's skinnin' the critter. You want to come up here an' wait for him?"

Skip agreed, and with Mrs. Baker's permission, he took Penny along. As they drove, the girl talked about the otter they had freed from the trap.

"I keep worrying about the poor thing," she said. "If he's lost a foot, I wonder if he'll be able to swim, and catch fish, and play the way he was doing in those pictures you took. Did you tell the game warden about the trap?"

"No," Skip admitted. "I clean forgot. He was in a hurry to put his dogs on the bear's trail an' didn't seem in the mood to talk. Maybe I'll have a chance to mention it if we see him tonight."

"I hope you will," said Penny. "That character up there in the woods may have it in for you, and I'd hate it if you got hurt."

They reached the Lukens' farm a few minutes later. It was dark, but Skip could make out the warden's station wagon in the yard. As he pulled up beside it, he heard the whimper of tired hounds in the rear of the car. Mr. Blake himself must be in the house. The door opened as they went up the steps, and he was standing there talking to Joe's father.

"Well," he said, "I reckon you folks won't be bothered any more. Wouldn't be surprised if I hit him with my second shot, but it was getting too dark to follow, and he was really high-tailing it north. Probably in New York State by now. Good night, all!"

He turned and met the boy and girl as they came in the door.

"Evening, Mr. Blake," said Skip. "I've got a picture of the bear here, if you'd like to see it."

There was a lamp on the table, and everybody gathered around to see the print.

"That's him, all right," the warden commented. "I caught a glimpse of that white nose this afternoon. Real good-sized bear, likely eight or ten years old. That must be a pretty slick arrangement you've got for taking night pictures!"

He turned toward the door again, obviously ready to start for home, but Penny stopped him.

"Mr. Blake," she said, "is it legal to set traps in the woods?"

"Depends on the time of year and what folks are trapping."

"Last week," she told him, "Skip and I found an otter caught in a trap, over back of the mountain. We let it go."

"Hmm," said the warden, frowning. "That sounds like trouble. Any idea who set the trap?"

"We think so," Skip put in. "At least we know there's a fairly big man up there who wears moccasins part of the time an' seems not to want anybody else around. He upset my rattrap arrangement when I had it fixed to take a night picture of a deer. 'Course, he didn't damage the camera, but we figure he's the one that set the otter trap."

"Keep your eyes peeled," said Blake. "I'll be watching for him, too, but if you see anybody who acts suspicious, let me know."

Chapter Six

That week Skip was full of plans for getting more animal pictures. Joe Lukens was no longer critical of the project. In fact, now that he had his bees in their winter boxes, he offered to help in any way he could.

"Well," Skip told him, "we know there are other animals around, like foxes an' coons. I thought I had a shot of a coon but got a 'possum instead—which is fine. Likely there are more animals prowling around at night. The only trouble is, I hate to go off an' leave the flash camera in the woods after what happened that first time."

"Heck," said Joe, "it's not very cold yet. Why couldn't we stay right near the camera some night? We could carry along a sleeping bag an' take turns watching."

The idea appealed to Skip. "Next good clear night we'll try it, if our folks say it's all right. You bring the sleeping bag, an' I'll pack some sandwiches. Let's make it Tuesday night if the weather's fair."

He asked his father for permission to spend a night in the woods with Joe, and John Rollins told him he could. "Just so you don't take any firearms," he said, "I guess you and Joe'll make out all right. Dress warm, though. It's likely to get pretty frosty up there."

After school on Tuesday, the two boys packed their equipment in Skip's old car and set out. They wanted enough daylight to look around for game trails and set up the camera. Skip parked on the south shoulder of the mountain where he had been before. They went in by the old lumber trail and climbed up through the brush, carrying the Graflex, tripod, and sleeping bag. The hillside was steep there, strewn with fallen trees, brush, and boulders. But after half an hour's scouting, Skip discovered a path that led along the slope. It was not man-made, he was sure. Hoofs and paws had followed it, skirting the rocks and thickets.

They picked a fairly level place in the trail and were about to set up the camera when Joe nudged Skip's arm. He pointed to a spot a few yards down the path. There, hardly visible, was a cleverly arranged rabbit snare made of thin wire. A birch sapling had been bent over and lightly held in place, so that any animal coming along the path would enter the noose and be jerked upward by the spring of the tree.

"Gee!" Joe whispered. "You s'pose that thing was set by your mystery man?"

"I shouldn't wonder," Skip replied with a frown. "Maybe if we fix up the camera right, we can get a picture of him. Are you game?"

"Sure! I guess the two of us can handle him. One thing, though—I'm goin' to cut me a good stout club."

They placed the Graflex carefully, partly hidden by a bush but with a clear view of the path and the snare. Then Joe checked on the direction of the breeze.

"We ought to get downwind, so an animal won't catch our scent," he said. "Then we can stay hid an' see what happens."

Since he intended to be on watch, Skip didn't bother to rig the rattrap for this shot. Instead, he kept the end of the black thread in his hand, so that he could set off the flash and trip the shutter from his place of concealment.

By that time it was well after sunset, and the woods were getting dark. The boys made themselves as comfortable as they could, ate some sandwiches, and drank hot cocoa from a Thermos bottle. They were sitting with their backs to a tree a few feet behind the camera. One thing Joe had remembered to bring was a flashlight, but there was no need to use it yet.

"Well," said Joe with a yawn, "who gets the first watch?"

Skip had a feeling that if anything happened, it would be after midnight. But Joe was obviously sleepy, so he decided to let him rest now and take the early morning watch.

"Go ahead," he said. "Crawl in the bag an' keep it warm for me. I'll wake you up about twelve o'clock."

Within five minutes the farm boy was sleeping soundly. Skip sat back and listened to the shush-shushing of the wind in the pines. It was a drowsy sound, yet he felt tensely alert. His ears were tuned to catch the small night noises of woods creatures, out of their dens and moving about in search of food now that daylight was gone.

Once he was startled by a sudden loud cry. *"Hoo!"* it came hoarsely. *"Hoo! Hoo-hoo!"* It was almost like a bark, but he knew it must have come from one of the big owls—a barred owl, probably, or even a great horned owl. His guess was proved right when a huge dark shape drifted silently past overhead.

After that there was a time of complete stillness, as the smaller animals cowered where they were, afraid to move under the keen eyes of the hunter. Nearly half an hour passed before they began to stir again. Meanwhile, the temperature was dropping steadily. Even in his ski pants, heavy sweater, and mackinaw, Skip was shivering. His muscles felt cramped, too, from sitting in one position.

He tied the end of the thread around the flashlight and laid it down softly so that he could stretch his arms and legs. Then he resumed his vigil, envying Joe the comfort of the sleeping bag.

To keep awake, as the hours dragged by, Skip silently repeated things he had learned by heart—the Twenty-third Psalm, "Paul Revere's Ride," the Gettysburg Address. By eleven o'clock he had exhausted all his small store of verse and prose. Every few minutes his eyelids drooped, and he had to jerk his attention back from the edge of sleep.

He was hardly aware of any sound, but something made him stare toward the spot in the trail where the snare was set. There was a faint twang of wire and a *whish* as the birch sprang erect. Half automatically, Skip pulled on the thread. The woods were lit by a flare of white light that lasted only a fraction of a second.

He scrambled to his feet and pushed on the button of the flashlight. There, dangling a yard or so above the trail, he saw the body of a good-sized cottontail rabbit, its neck fast in the wire noose. The sudden light had roused the sleeping Joe. Now he came stumbling out of the bag, asking what had happened.

"A rabbit came along the trail an' got caught in the snare," Skip told him. "What I'm going to do is reset the camera an' put in a fresh bulb. Then we'll be ready for the poacher if he comes before daylight. How about it—you want to stand watch for a spell?"

"Sure," said Joe, rubbing his eyes. "I had a nap all right, even if it did seem pretty short."

Joe took the end of the thread and settled back against the tree while Skip crawled into the warm sleeping bag. Delightful as it felt after the sharp night air, he couldn't seem to fall asleep. He was worrying about Joe and wondering if he would stay alert.

In any case, Skip was wide awake half an hour later when there was a sudden commotion on the path. The camera flash went off, and in its momentary light he saw a big catlike animal leap away with half the rabbit in its teeth.

"Wh-what was it?" Joe asked. "Could you see?"

"Looked like a big bobcat to me. Anyhow, the picture'll tell us. Boy—this has been quite a night! I'd just as soon wait an' try to catch the fellow that set the snare some other time. Let's go home an' get some real sleep."

Joe was more than willing, for he had already grown stiff with the cold. They lugged their equipment back to the car and drove down the mountain. By one o'clock they were both in their own beds.

* * *

Skip felt a little ashamed the next morning. If they had had a bit more endurance, they might have waited it out and possibly nabbed or photographed the poacher. On the other hand, it had been a lot colder on the mountain than he had expected. They might both have come down with pneumonia if they had stayed.

He called Tom Blake that evening and told him about the rabbit snare and the bobcat. The warden was interested enough to ask a lot of questions.

"I won't rest easy," he said, "till I've brought that fellow in and seen him sentenced. Think you got a good shot o' the cat?"

"It's hard to tell," Skip replied. "Joe pulled the shutter an' he was pretty excited. I'll try to finish the film an' develop it this weekend. Then I'll know."

He had hardly hung up the receiver when Elmer Hunt drove up to the front of the house. He jumped out of the station wagon and ran to the steps.

"Hey, Skip," he exclaimed when the door was opened. "My two brothers are goin' on a coon hunt tonight. Want to come?"

"Gee," said Skip, "I'd sure like to, but Joe an' I were up on the mountain last night an' didn't get much sleep. How long do you reckon we'll be out?"

"Oh, not long! We know where there's some coons, an' Bill's borrowed a real good coon hound. Bring along your camera. You might get a picture for your project."

"All right. When are you starting?"

"About an hour. You be ready an' we'll pick you up."

It was seven-thirty then. Skip rushed through his home-work and got into his warmest outdoor clothes. The Graflex would be the camera to use, he thought, and he put a couple of spare flash bulbs in his pocket.

Mrs. Rollins was unhappy about his going out two nights in a row, but he assured her he would probably be home long before midnight. Then he sat down on the front steps to wait. The Hunts must have been delayed, for it was al-most nine when their car drove up. Elmer's older brothers, Bill and Lew, were in the front seat. Skip got into the second seat with Elmer, and still farther back in the station wagon, he could hear the snuffle and whimper of a dog.

"This here's Rowser," Elmer said. "He belongs to a neigh-bor, an' they claim he's the best coon dog in Hickory County. Half hound an' half Airedale. He's got a hound's nose for trailin' an' a terrier's yen for a fight."

The car went through town and followed the Creek Road north along the Blacksnake for two or three miles. There were thick woods there in the bottom lands, and it was into a patch of these woods that the station wagon turned. After a few hundred yards, the trail petered out.

"Here we are," Bill Hunt announced. "You boys stay back of us now, an' go quiet."

He carried a rifle, and Lew had a shotgun. As soon as Rowser was let out of the car, the dog started a businesslike search of the ground under the trees. Using a flashlight occa-sionally, they could see him quartering through the brush, his nose down, sniffing for a scent.

Nothing happened for a while. Then a hesitant, mournful sound came from the dog's throat. He repeated it more confidently. Now he was running, in full cry, on a hot trail.

"Come on!" Lew urged. "Got to keep near enough to hear him when he trees the critter!"

The chase led deeper into the woods, angling toward the swampy ground along the stream. Even with the flashlight to guide them, it was hard going. Carrying the big camera and trying to protect it from whipping brush was real work, and Skip was soon panting for breath.

At last the voice of the dog, ahead, changed from baying to an excited bark. Lew, who was in the lead with the flashlight, pointed it up into a big oak tree and let out a whoop.

"There he is!" he called. "A big old he-coon, up in the second crotch! See him?"

"Wait!" gasped Skip as he hurried closer. "Let me get a picture before you shoot him!"

He unlimbered the camera and aimed upward at the crouching animal. In the light of the electric torch, he could see the coon's face plainly—the black bandit-mask and the bared teeth. He centered it in the finder and pressed the button.

The bulb went off with a satisfying flash, and at the startling glare, the raccoon hastily scrambled higher.

"Can you see him, Bill?" Lew asked. "I'll hold the light on him, an' you take a shot."

"O.K.," Bill replied. "Here goes!"

When the rifle cracked, they saw bark fly from the limb where the coon was perched. Then the animal jumped. He came sailing down, spread out like a flying squirrel, and landed almost at their feet.

"Get him, Rowser!" yelled Elmer, but the command was hardly needed. The dog knew his job. For a moment there was a wild scuffle of snarling, snapping coon and battling hound. Then Rowser emerged with the beast's sagging body in his jaws. He had caught it by the scruff of the neck and broken its back with one mighty jerk.

"Whew!" Skip breathed. "That was quick!"

They examined the dead coon and found the scar of Bill's bullet in its shoulder. "Not a very clean shot," the older brother admitted. "Reckon he'd ha' got away if Rowser hadn't been along. Yes, sir, boy—you're quite a dog!"

64

The fur was in fair condition, and Bill took the coon home to skin it. "Maybe we can make a real Dan'l Boone cap out of him!" He grinned.

When they let Skip out at his door, he was surprised to see lights still on in the house. Then he heard the courthouse clock strike the hour. In spite of all that had happened, it was only eleven o'clock!

Chapter Seven

Taking stock of that week's work, Skip couldn't help feeling a bit proud of himself. He finished the exposures on the Graflex film pack and started developing them as soon as possible. The weekly 4-H meeting would be at Penny Baker's that Friday night, and he wanted to have some more prints to show the club.

By working in the darkroom after school and again after supper, he managed to finish in time. With the prints in a big envelope, he hurried over to Penny's and arrived only three minutes late.

"Got a new rule," announced Dutch Krouse. "Anybody that ain't on time has to stand the rest of us a malted at the drugstore."

If Skip hadn't seen him wink at the other boys, he might have believed it.

"Oh, well," he said with a laugh, "as long as I'm new around here, I guess you'll let it go this time. Besides, I've got a good excuse." He pointed to the envelope.

"Don't tell me you expect to report on your durn animals again!" Krouse groaned. "That's just for the monthly meetings. Tonight we're here to have fun."

"Now you look here, Dutch," Penny told him sternly. "The fun can come later. At these weekly meetings we're supposed to help each other with our projects first. Maybe Skip needs help. As far as I'm concerned, I'd like to see what he's got."

"Me, too," said Joe. "I want another look at the wildcat we saw." And his interest was quickly echoed by Elmer Hunt, who wanted to know how the picture of the raccoon had turned out.

Five minutes later they were all gathered around the table, where Skip spread his prints out under the lamp. The one of the coon wasn't as clear as he would have liked, for he had had to hold the big camera at a difficult angle. But the animal's face showed sharp above the oak bough, and there was no question about its identity.

Next he came to the rabbit in the snare. At the moment he had set off the flash, the poor beast was being jerked violently upward, so there was some blurring on the film. Joe had done better with his shot. The cat was caught almost at the top of its leap, with the hindquarters of the rabbit half torn away.

"Hey—look at the size of that feller!" Elmer exclaimed. "Skip, that's no ordinary bobcat. He's got whiskers of hair on his ears. I bet that's a Canada lynx!"

After some argument among the boys, Penny produced a volume of her father's encyclopedia. Several types of wildcats and lynxes were shown, from the smaller grayish bobcat and the *Lynx rufus* to the big *Lynx canadensis*. The long legs, large paws, and stubby tail looked convincing, but the clincher seemed to be the hairy tufts on the ears.

Because he wanted to be certain, Skip called the game warden early the next morning. Blake was just starting for the other side of the mountain, but he agreed to stop by the Rollins's house on his way.

"What's all this?" he asked when Skip met him at the door. "You boys think you got a picture of a Canada lynx? I never heard of one bein' seen south of the Adirondacks, but let's have a look at your photograph."

He studied the print for some time. "I could tell better if he was standin' on all four feet," he said at last. "But I'll admit he looks pretty big for a bobcat. More hair at the tips o' the ears, too. Now if you'd told me you'd spotted a mountain lion, I'd believe it quicker. Twenty years ago, when I was a kid your age, there was a panther killed not ten miles from here. But a Canada lynx! A book I've got says they've been extinct in Pennsylvania for sixty years. I'd better check with the Game Commission."

"I wish you would," said Skip. "And I'll make a couple more prints, so you can send 'em one. I sure hope they can tell us. Whatever the animal is, I have to know for my 4-H project."

*   *   *

It was nearly the middle of October now, and there was a rime of frost on the grass nearly every morning. The farmers had their apples picked and their root crops in. Most of the corn had been laid away in the cribs, and the stubble fields were golden with rows of fat pumpkins.

Much of the talk at school and in the 4-H Club meetings was about the Hickory County Fair. It was to be held the coming Saturday, at the old fairgrounds, south of town. Skip was almost as interested in Joe's and Elmer's entries as if he were going to have an exhibit himself.

On Friday night the trucks were rolling down the highway, carrying pigs, calves, sheep, and chickens to the big livestock building, where the judging would take place. Skip saw Dutch Krouse go by with his mammoth pig well bedded in straw in the stake truck.

"Hi!" Dutch yelled. "I'm goin' to bring home a blue ribbon with ol' Goliath, here!"

Despite his dislike of bragging, Skip hoped that boast was right, for he knew the big hog was Dutch's pride and joy. Then he remembered the way the other boy had made fun of his own wildlife project. As he recalled it, Dutch had offered to eat any animals he got over ten. Counting on his fingers, he was pretty sure the total was now eleven, and he grinned to himself as he thought of bringing that to Krouse's attention. He hoped Dutch's appetite was good.

Everybody got up early on Fair Day. Skip hurried through his breakfast and, driving Abigail, joined the line of cars headed for the grounds. While he was finding a parking place, he ran into Penny Baker, whose arms were full of jars of preserves.

"Hey!" She laughed. "Give me a hand, will you, Skip? You'll find some more of my goodies in the back seat."

He helped her carry the preserves into the Home Arts Building and arrange them on one of the display shelves. Across the aisle they saw Joe Lukens, bending lovingly above his jars of strained honey and boxes of honey in the comb. Most of the people in the building at that early hour were those who had brought entries, and the big crowds wouldn't arrive till later in the day.

Joe greeted Penny and Skip with a grin. "Your stuff all set up?" he asked. "So's mine. Let's go over an' look down our noses at the livestock exhibits. I saw Elmer come in with his calf, an' I heard Dutch slept right in the pen with that over-grown hog of his!"

A chorus of barnyard sounds came to their ears as they crossed the Midway to the Livestock Building. Cattle were bellowing and roosters crowing, and beneath the uproar there was a steady, contented sound of animals munching on their feed.

Dutch Krouse's pig, farrowed the previous spring, was a big red Duroc, so fat it could hardly waddle. Dutch was in the pen with it now, brushing and currying with frowning concentration. When they hailed him, he merely grunted in response. There were seven or eight other pens of swine, and in one of them Joe saw a 4-H boy he knew who lived on a farm at the upper end of the county.

"That's Jed Monroe," said Joe, and took his companions

over to introduce them. Jed was a lanky youngster with a shy grin. He, too, was grooming a pig—a sleek black Hampshire with a broad band of white around the forward part of its chunky body.

"Oh, what a beauty!" Penny exclaimed. "I never thought a pig could be so handsome!"

"It's sort of a pretty breed," Jed admitted. "The white stripe makes 'em look different, anyhow. Don't grow quite as big as some, but they make mighty good hams an' bacon."

They wished him luck in the judging and moved on to the dairy-cattle section. Three of their own club members were busy there with their calves—a Holstein, a Brown Swiss, and Elmer's Guernsey. She was a beautiful little creature, with the slim legs and great brown eyes of a deer. Her coat was a pattern of rich golden-brown and white, and her build showed the pure-bred lines of her famous parentage.

"Boy!" said Joe Lukens. "If you don't win with her, some of the judges sure need new glasses!"

Elmer looked pleased. "Well, I'm hoping," he replied. "There's some other good calves here, though."

The poultry was housed in an annex to the main building. There they found more 4-H boys and girls readying their exhibits. One was showing pouter pigeons, another ducks, and several had brought cockerels and pullets of the better-known breeds.

"We'd better get back," Penny told the boys. "They always judge the jams and jellies and baked goods before lunch. I guess they want their taste buds to be sharp."

Quite a crowd had now gathered in the Home Arts Building, and the three judges were already preparing their pencils and notebooks. One was a hotelkeeper, another the leading grocer in Welbyville, and the third was a quiet little middle-aged housewife. They started with the pies and bread, voting ribbons in each class. It took nearly an hour for them to reach the cakes and cookies.

"Well, I guess it won't be long now," Joe whispered nervously. "I hope the pickles won't kill their taste for sweet stuff."

The judges were moving toward them, and a half-smothered belch from the hotel man did little to dispel Joe's worries. Only three other beekeepers had entered honey in the competition, and as Skip pointed out, his friend was pretty sure to get a ribbon of some kind.

"Hm," they heard the grocer remark. "Honey, eh? This here's a mighty nice-lookin' piece o' comb."

He took a knife and cut one corner of Joe's exhibit and put it, dripping, in his mouth.

"Good, too!" he commented. "Try some, Mrs. Foster."

She took a taste and closed her eyes. "Fall honey," she pronounced. "Buckwheat an' goldenrod." And she made a note on the paper she carried.

They tested the jars of strained honey next, then went into a huddle. It took only a moment or two for them to reach a decision, and Skip saw the grocer advance toward the shelves with three ribbons in his hand. The blue went to Joe Lukens' entry.

"Yippee!" Skip exclaimed. "You made it! First prize!"

There were, of course, no names on any of the exhibits, but Skip was pretty sure he could pick Penny's entries out of the long rows of gleaming glass, rich with the reds and purples of carefully preserved fruit.

It was Mrs. Foster who appeared to be taking command at this point. The men judges stood back a step and let her work. First she checked the translucent color and appearance of the jellies, then tried their flavor on the tip of a teaspoon.

"Now whoever made this," she said, pursing her lips, "put in a little too much sugar an' cooked it a mite long. It's a shame. Used nice grapes, too."

So it went as she moved down the line. One was too tart, another lacking in flavor. At last she came to Penny's jelly, and Skip held his breath. Mrs. Foster lifted the glass up to the light, sampled the contents, and smiled.

"Here's one woman knows how to do it," she said. "You gentlemen try a little an' tell me if you ever tasted better red-currant jelly."

The male judges instantly concurred. Before they finished, Penny had walked off with two firsts in jellies and a second for strawberry jam. She took it calmly, but the boys could hardly contain themselves.

"Just for that," said Skip, "I'll treat you both to lunch. It's past noon anyway."

They found space at a busy counter and ate hamburgers, washed down with tall, cold shakes. Then they wandered across to see what was happening in the Livestock Building. The largest crowds were gathered in the dairy-calf section. There was only one judge working here—an elderly professor of animal husbandry from the State University. He was a gray, wrinkled little man, but his keen eyes and knowing hands took in every detail of the animals before him.

Quietly he examined the Brown Swiss, the Holstein, and two or three other calves. Then he came to Elmer's Guernsey heifer. She stood beautifully, with no sign of nervousness. Every inch of her glowed from her young owner's grooming. But it was the fine straight line of her back, the shape of her hips, and the carriage of her head that took most of the judge's attention.

When he handed the blue ribbon to Elmer, the crowd voiced hearty approval. And the 4-H members were pleased to see the other two club entries take second and third places.

It was the same judge who now walked toward the pens where the swine were quartered. Dutch Krouse, red-faced from currying his huge pig, grinned confidently at the man's approach. There were twelve entries in this division, and it took some time for the little professor to observe them all.

He paused longest before two pens—Dutch's and Jed Monroe's.

After that, each pig was put on the scales. To nobody's surprise, the fat Duroc weighed 445 pounds, nearly 50 pounds more than the next heaviest entry. Dutch was really beaming now. The judge stroked his chin for a full minute before he went back to the table and got his ribbons.

"Son," he told Dutch kindly, "this may be a shock to you,

but your pig gets second place. I know he's the heaviest. What you've done is to overfeed him and give him too little exercise. He'd make plenty of lard but not enough solid meat. Here's your red ribbon and remember that next year."

Dutch looked so thunderstruck that Skip couldn't help feeling sorry for him. He collapsed heavily on a box in the pen while the judge was presenting the winner's ribbon to Jed Monroe and his Hampshire.

Penny went over to Dutch's side and put a hand on his shoulder. "Don't feel bad," she told him quietly. "A second place is something you can be proud of."

"Aw, leave me alone," he mumbled, close to tears.

"Too bad," said Joe Lukens as they walked away. "Old Dutch hates to lose at anything. I sure hope he listened to what the judge said. A fellow has to learn from his mistakes."

Chapter Eight

There came a time, in mid-October, when a wave of Indian summer swept up the valley. A gentle south wind blew for days on end, the sky was a hazy blue, and the sun glowed softly on the russet and gold of oaks and hickories.

Skip thought the chance was too good to miss. On Saturday he put a roll of color film in the Retina and drove up the mountain, hoping for some animal pictures but willing to settle for a day in the open. This time he took a road over the south shoulder and on around to the western slope. It was wild country back there, thickly forested, with only one or two little farms breaking the miles of evergreen and hardwood growth.

He parked Abigail at the edge of the rocky track and climbed up through a grove of pines. His feet made no noise in the soft brown needles that covered the ground. But there were other sounds—the little chirpings and scurryings of birds and small animals. Then he heard a different noise. It was a booming like a muffled drum, and it seemed to come from a pine clump just ahead. Skip screwed the zoom lens on the camera and held it ready as he crept forward.

He made the last few yards on his hands and knees, peering ahead through the pine boughs. The drumming was louder now, and his heart beat faster, for he thought he knew what it was. Sure enough, as he came to the edge of the thicket, he saw a ruffed grouse perched on a hollow log. Its neck feathers were extended, and its wings were beating so rapidly against its body that they looked like a blur. Very carefully Skip sighted the camera and clicked the shutter. At the faint sound, the bird launched itself upward and took off with a thunder of wings.

Skip was sorry to disturb it when it appeared to be having so much fun, but he thought he had an unusual picture. Some time, he decided, when he had finished with the animals of Hickory County, he would have to start on a similar project dealing with game birds.

The sun was warm and the air drowsy there in the little glade where the grouse had been drumming. Skip sat down with his back against a tree. The camera was ready in his lap, but he was content just to enjoy the quiet of the woods. His eyes closed, and in another moment he would almost surely have been asleep.

Then the silence was broken by a sudden chattering. He looked up to see a big gray squirrel, its cheeks bulging with nuts of some kind, trying to reach its nest in a nearby oak. The way was barred by a red squirrel only half the size of the gray but twice as pugnacious. And they were far too busy with their feud to notice the boy on the ground.

He aimed the camera, waited till they were both in plain view and close together, then pressed the shutter button. Two more animals to add to his collection!

His sympathies were with the gray squirrel, and he stood up and hurled a stick toward the combatants. At once the smaller and noisier animal whisked away to the upper branches, and the gray scrambled safely to its hole.

Skip no longer felt sleepy. He decided to push on and explore more of this side of the mountain, where he had never been. The climbing grew steeper, and soon he came to a jumble of rocks at the foot of a high ledge. It looked grim and forbidding until suddenly, as he watched, the noon sun came over the cliff and fell in golden warmth on the gray boulders. He moved slowly along, looking up at the face of the ledge. As he half expected, there was a break in the granite surface, and he saw what looked like the entrance to a small cave. There was an attraction about it he could hardly resist. Without a second's hesitation, he started clambering up over the rocks.

When he was within two or three yards of the cave's mouth, he saw something that stopped him in his tracks. There on the top of a flat boulder was the biggest, fattest rattlesnake he had ever seen!

Hardly daring to breathe, Skip raised the camera, set it for six feet, and clicked the shutter. The big snake moved then. It had been lying stretched out on the stony surface, enjoying the sun's warmth. Now it coiled quickly, head lifted and tail in motion, giving a dry, warning *whir*. Skip was scared now, but he waited for one more shot before retreating. When he reached a safe distance, he set the camera down and picked up a rock that weighed four or five pounds. Taking careful aim, he pitched it as hard as he could at the snake's hissing head.

The stone missed its target by an inch or two but struck the coiled body a heavy blow. For an instant there was a writhing and twisting of the mottled brown skin. Then the huge rattler was in fluid motion, gliding swiftly up into the cave entrance, and all Skip's desire to explore that particular cavern had left him.

He watched the ground ahead of him with care as he went back down the mountainside. Where one snake was, there might be others. A few copperheads had been found in the county as well as rattlers, and weather like this would be likely to bring them out.

Finally he reached the little woods road and the car. While he ate the sandwiches he had brought along, he thought about that cave in the ledge. There had been a wild idea in his mind, when he first saw the place, that this might be the hideout of the mysterious trapper. The presence of the snake had quickly dispelled that thought, but where, he wondered, could such a man live and sleep if not in a cave? There might be other caves, of course. Or he could have built himself some kind of hidden shelter, deep in the woods, where even the deer hunters would fail to find him. That didn't seem very likely, however, for when the season opened, late in November, the mountain fairly swarmed with red-capped and red-coated men looking for deer.

Earlier that morning he had come across a little rivulet of water running down a gully in the slope. When he had finished eating, he traced the tiny stream back to its source and drank at the spring, where the water bubbled out of the rocks. In the moss, there at the edge, he saw other footprints, but they were so blurred and irregular that it was impossible to tell whether a man or an animal had made them. He turned slowly around, scanning the ground behind him. Was he mistaken, or had he found a trace of a path through the brush? If it was a path, it seemed to come angling down to the spring from higher ground.

Skip drew a deep breath and started to follow it. Soon he was almost certain no man had made that trail, for within a few yards it disappeared under a thick curtain of bushes that intertwined a scant foot above the ground. Rabbits, perhaps, or some other small animal? He skirted around the thicket, and there was the faint trail once more.

The excitement of discovery gripped him now. He resolved not to turn back until he knew more about the creatures that came to drink at the spring. The sun felt hot on his back as he toiled up the mountainside. There was no cooling shade here, for he was in a belt of hardwoods, where most of the leaves had fallen. Twice he lost the little path, only to find it again after minutes of searching.

Finally Skip sat down on a root and wiped his dripping forehead. It was as hot as midsummer, and he was dressed for an autumn day. There was no wind at all. From where he sat, he had a fairly good view up the slope, and just as he was about to get to his feet again, he saw something move up there.

He remained perfectly still, staring at the place, fifty yards away and some distance above him. Perhaps his eyes had played him a trick. All he could see now was a mound of yellowish earth near the foot of a large tree. Then a little yellow-brown lump, just the color of the ground, tumbled down the slope and quickly crawled back again. Skip breathed faster. The thing that had moved looked like a tiny yellow puppy. He set the camera for a fairly long shot and started creeping higher, careful to make no noise.

It must have taken him ten minutes to negotiate twenty yards. At times his view was obscured by brush, but he didn't mind that, for it meant he, too, was concealed. At last he reached a place where he could peer under a laurel bush and see the mound of earth again. And this time he was near enough to make out the little black eyes and nose tips of a pair of baby foxes, playing there in the dirt in front of their den. He lay flat, resting on his elbows, and focused the Retina on the darker opening above them, just at the base of the tree.

Should he risk a shot of the kits or wait and hope their mother would come out? She might not be in the den at all, of course, but off foraging somewhere. He made his decision, held his eye to the finder until both the little fellows were clearly visible, then clicked the shutter.

The baby foxes didn't seem to notice the sound at all, but keener ears heard it. Just as Skip pulled the lever that brought the next frame into place, the head of a fine red fox appeared above the hole. She was beautifully silhouetted against the dark pine trunk, and he knew he had a good picture the moment he snapped it.

Less than a second later, the mother fox and her two kits had vanished into their den, but Skip was happy. He had had a pretty successful day.

*   *   *

On the way home he stopped to take more shots of the mountain scenery, for he was anxious now to finish his film and get it processed in time for the next 4-H meeting—the monthly one where they would report on their projects.

He hurried to the post office and mailed the film that afternoon. Then he drove out to the Lukens' farm to see Joe.

"Gosh!" the other boy exclaimed when he heard Skip's account of what had happened. "I sure wish I'd been with you! Maybe we could have killed that snake. A set of rattles like those would be a mighty good souvenir."

"I wish I'd killed him, too," Skip agreed. "The skin would make a nice belt or a trophy to nail up on the wall. But, anyhow, I'm sure I got his picture—a good close-up, too."

"Those foxes must have been pretty to watch," said Joe. "They do a lot of damage, though. You didn't notice any feathers or chicken bones around, did you? Somethin's been raidin' our henhouse the last couple of nights, an' I wouldn't be surprised if it was that fox you saw."

"I didn't get close enough to notice any feathers," Skip replied. "I figured I might want to go back for more pictures later, an' didn't want to scare 'em too much. But why don't we rig up the big camera an' try for a night shot of your chicken thief?"

Joe was doubtful about getting his father's permission. "I heard him vow he'd shoot the rascal," he said, "even if he has to sit up all night tonight with a gun."

"Well," said Skip, "it won't hurt if I ask him, will it? He seemed to be pretty interested the time we got a picture of the bear."

They found Joe's father in the barn, and Skip made his suggestion.

"Go ahead," Mr. Lukens told them. "I don't hanker to lose a whole night's sleep, an' I guess that flash would scare the fox away about as well as a gunshot. I'll show you where the critter's been gettin' in."

They followed him out to the wire-enclosed run beside the chicken house, and he pointed to a place where some animal had dug a hole under the wire.

"I've filled it in with rocks an' dirt twice," he said, "but that don't seem to stop him. Just tunnels it out again."

"How big was the hole?" Skip asked.

"Oh, six inches deep, maybe. Big enough for a skinny fox to squeeze under without much trouble. Why don't you rig up your camera right over here an' put the rattrap where he's sure to start diggin'?"

With this encouragement Skip drove home and brought back the Graflex and its equipment. It was growing dark when he and Joe finished setting the trap, making sure the thread was taut, and positioning the camera.

"Call me up first thing in the morning if we get anything," Skip told his friend. "I'll set my alarm for seven o'clock, so I'll be ready to answer."

He reached home just as dinner was put on the table. "Where have you been all day?" his father asked, and it took him most of the next half hour to tell of his adventures on the mountain. Mrs. Rollins began to worry as soon as she heard about the rattlesnake.

"My goodness!" she exclaimed. "I don't know as I like you going up there all alone. Suppose that snake had bitten you! John, shouldn't we put a stop to this?"

"Oh, I guess he's able to take care of himself," Skip's father replied with a reassuring grin. "This warm weather won't last long, and all the snakes'll hole up for the winter as soon as it gets cold. I know how much fun a boy can have cruising around in the woods. Used to do it myself. You'll be careful, won't you, son?"

"Of course," said Skip. "An', Mom, if it'll make you feel any better, I'll carry a snake-bite kit in the car. You sell 'em, don't you, Dad?"

Before he went to bed, he explained about the possibility of an early phone call from Joe Lukens. "If you hear it ring," he said, "just go back to sleep. I may go out to the farm, but I'll be back in time for breakfast."

The alarm woke him at seven, and he turned it off, jumping out of bed and pulling on his clothes. The room was cold. During the night a north wind had sprung up, and the Indian summer weather was over. Shivering, Skip tiptoed downstairs and waited by the telephone. Time passed but nothing happened. After a while his mother came down to start breakfast, and still Joe hadn't called.

It was eight-thirty and Skip was eating his second stack of pancakes when the phone jingled. Joe's voice came to him, half strangled with laughter.

"Skip"—he was chuckling—"the camera went off all right. But you'd better not come till after church. When you do come, wear the oldest clothes you've got!"

"Why?" asked Skip, mystified. Then the truth dawned on him. "Oh, no!" he gasped. "You mean the fox turned out to be a skunk?"

"That's right. When that flash went off, he must ha' been really scared. Sprayed everything in sight. But he didn't get into the chicken run!"

Chapter Nine

Skip took his friend's advice and changed into old clothes as soon as he came home from church. Then, with some misgivings, he drove to the Lukens' farm. Joe was waiting for him in the barnyard.

"I guess it isn't really as bad as I told you." He grinned. "But you can smell skunk, even from here."

It was true—the musky odor still hung in the air. Cautiously they made their way to the wire fence outside the henhouse. With a couple of sticks, Skip picked up the sprung trap, which appeared to have been the chief object of the skunk's indignation. He carried it at arm's length to an old, discarded bucket that stood under the barn eaves and was half full of water.

"Have to let it soak a while," he said. "Maybe I can find another one or try to disinfect this when I get it home."

The camera, fortunately, had not been in the direct line of fire. A slight scent clung about it, but Skip took it off the tripod and deposited both in the rear of the car.

"Well," he told Joe, "as far as my project goes, this is a real help. If the picture turns out all right, it gives me still another animal."

"How many you got now?"

"Wait, let me count. At the start I took pictures of the buck deer in the old apple orchard, and the groundhog and the weasel and field mouse. That's four. Then I got a shot of a chipmunk, and the 'possum in Dad's corn patch. Six. Then there was the otter, and the bear robbing your hives—eight. An' the night you and I spent in the woods, we got the rabbit and the lynx. Right after that there was the coon—that makes eleven. Yesterday I took pictures of a gray squirrel and a red one, besides the foxes. And now a skunk. Gives me a count of fifteen, leaving out the rattler."

"Gee!" said Joe, impressed. "Sure is a lot more'n I expected when you started. But I guess you're about finished now."

Skip laughed. "I wouldn't bet on that," he said. "I've still got all winter ahead, so I might find one or two more."

Actually he was far from sure. Perhaps there were other animals in the woods, but he found it hard to think of any. And soon the snow would make traveling more difficult up there on the mountain.

By Friday night he had his new pictures ready for the 4-H meeting. The flash shot of the skunk was one of his best, helped by the clear white stripe on the animal's black back. It had been taken just as the skunk started digging with its fore paws and before its artillery went into action. The color slides, too, were all he could ask, and he was especially proud of the fox family portrait. Loaded with his projector and screen, he drove to the Grange Hall.

There was a good crowd present that night. By eight o'clock nearly twenty-five boys and girls had assembled. The only conspicuous absentee was Dutch Krouse, still sulking after his hog's defeat. He finally arrived, twenty minutes late, and sat at the back of the room.

Meanwhile, the other club members had begun making their progress reports. The County Fair had wound up most of the boys' projects, with the judging of calves, lambs, pigs, and poultry. Joe Lukens was proud to display his blue ribbon for honey, and Elmer Hunt told of being offered eight hundred dollars for his heifer.

"Pa an' I decided we'd keep her," he said. "She'll be worth

more'n that to us. Ought to be the star o' the herd in a couple more years."

Penny, of course, drew applause for the ribbons she had
taken in the jams and jellies, but there were others who were
congratulated just as sincerely for lesser honors. The main
thing was that they had done their best, win or lose.

Finally Ed Jones, the club leader, asked young Krouse to
step up and give his report. For a moment Dutch hung back.
Then he strode forward with a scowl.

"I didn't come to be laughed at about my pig," he said. "I
want to resign from 4-H right now."

There was a shocked silence at first. Then Skip got up and
went toward the big German boy.

"Heck, Dutch," he said, "it wasn't your fault you didn't
win. That judge was just partial to Hampshires, I reckon.
You'd sure done a champion job fattenin' your pig an'
groomin' him."

"That's right, Dutch!" Penny spoke up. "Remember—my
strawberry jam came in second, too. But that doesn't mean
I'm quitting. Just wait till next year! We all know you can
raise a blue-ribbon pig."

Others would have joined in, but Cale Douglas, the
County Agent, raised his hand to quiet them.

"Dutch," he said, "I expect everybody feels the same way.
But we don't want to have to beg you to stay with the club.
If you've made up your own mind to quit, that's your privi-
lege. Just one thing, though—don't rush into this in too
much of a hurry. Think about it for a week, then resign if
you like. We won't hold it against you, and if you feel like
coming back into 4-H later, you'll be welcome."

The unhappy boy looked at the floor, undecided. At last
he agreed grudgingly. "O.K.," he said, "I'll wait till next
meetin'. It's s'posed to be at my house, anyhow. I wouldn't
want to cheat my mom out o' cookin' for you."

"Yea, Dutch!" Some of the boys cheered, and others went

over to shake his hand. There was a look of relief on all their faces.

When the crisis had passed and the meeting was called to order again, Skip heard his own name called.

"We're all interested in that wildlife project of yours," said the leader. "Maybe you've got some more animals to report on."

Skip carried the screen to the front of the room. "Yes, I have," he announced. "Dutch, I don't want to spoil your appetite for that good food your mother cooks, but maybe you remember saying you'd eat any animals I found above ten. Which'll you try—skunk or rattlesnake?"

There was a roar of laughter in which Dutch joined, somewhat sheepishly. Skip plugged in the projector and showed his color transparencies. The girls shivered and squealed at the sight of the rattler, coiled to strike, but a moment later they were *ooh*ing and *ah*ing over the pictures of the baby foxes. The two squirrels came next. Then he produced his black-and-white enlargement of the skunk, taken with the flash camera.

"I thought I smelled somethin' funny when you came in," called Joe Lukens. "Where'd you bury those clothes?"

Skip waited till the laughter died down. "Maybe my project's finished, too," he said. "Fifteen wild animals is more'n I I expected to get when I started. But I'll keep on trying. When the deer season starts, it'll be risky going up in the woods, but later in the winter I might be able to track something in the snow."

"Long as you've got pictures of way over the required number of animals," said Ed Jones, "you might start planning on something else."

He dug into his briefcase and pulled out two more pamphlets, similar to the one Skip had. "One of these is on birds and the other covers reptiles and amphibians. You've already taken shots of a hawk, a grouse, and a rattlesnake. Come spring, there'll be lots more birds. Snakes, too, and frogs and turtles and such. Want to try?"

"Sure thing!" Skip replied. "I was wondering what would come next, after I ran out of animals. Thanks!"

As usual, the meeting was followed by light refreshments and a square dance. As he whirled Penny in the jigging dance figures, Skip was happy to see that Dutch Krouse was also having a good time. His threat to drop out of the club seemed completely forgotten.

*   *   *

It rained that weekend, and Skip stayed indoors, working on his project book. Identifying the animals was only one part of the requirements. He had to put down the date and place where he had found each one; write what he knew about their food and habits; describe the dens or homes of at least five of them; and learn the state game laws as they applied to each species. In addition, he was supposed to prepare a chart showing whether the animal was beneficial to man or harmful.

In making up these charts, he arrived at some conclusions that surprised him. The groundhog was a fairly simple case. It was a grass and grain eater. It did a lot of damage to clover and other crops, and its burrows were a menace to haying machinery. On the favorable side he could find nothing at all to put down.

Checking up on opossums in a natural history book, he found a lot to intrigue him. They were marsupials—carried their babies in a pouch, like kangaroos. And they were one of the few American mammals with prehensile tails. Not much could be said in their favor except that they were interesting animals.

Field mice might be better, for he found they consumed a great many weed plants and some grubs and insects, as well as a small amount of good grass. The weasel was a real problem. He certainly helped to keep down the rodent population, but he was also a notorious chicken and egg thief, and he killed for the mere sake of killing. On balance, Skip decided the weasel wasn't worth protecting.

Foxes were perhaps unjustly considered in the same class, called enemies by all poultry farmers, though more than half their food was probably rabbits, mice, and crickets. Skunks almost certainly did more good than harm. They lived largely on beetles and grasshoppers, with only an occasional raid on a chicken yard.

Going back over the list, he realized that every wild creature he had photographed had its place in maintaining the balance of nature. Even bobcats did their part. Without them, the country might suddenly find itself knee-deep in rabbits. And rabbits, while harmless enough in their place, could probably eat more food crops in proportion to their weight than cattle or hogs!

The otter could hardly be classed as a marauder, except by the trout fishermen. He was such a playful, attractive animal and so rare in the district that Skip felt strongly he should be protected.

Another beautiful creature was the white-tailed deer. In spite of occasional damage done to farm crops, the countryside would be a lot poorer if there were no graceful bucks and does and fawns about. The game laws, which allowed deer hunting for a short period each fall, were really a benefit to the deer, as well as to the farmers and hunters. The open season kept the animals from multiplying too fast and dying of starvation.

Now he came to two puzzling characters—the black bear and his smaller cousin, the raccoon. What good were they in a modern world? Try as he would, he could think of no useful purpose they served. And yet he felt instinctively it would be a less interesting world without them.

Perhaps he ought to get a professional opinion, and the

natural person to turn to was the game warden, Tom Blake. Skip went to the phone and called his number and was lucky to find him at home. In answer to Skip's question, he chuckled.

"Bears don't bother me much," he said, "unless some farmer gets riled up about 'em. They're sort o' comical critters, an' unless they're wounded or protecting their cubs, they let men pretty much alone. To tell you the truth, I was shooting in the air that time up back of Lukens' place. All I wanted was to give the bear a scare. Better not tell Mr. Lukens, though."

"So," said Skip, "you think it's right that bears should be protected, except for a short hunting season?"

"Yep. You can quote me on that. An' by the way, I've got a letter back from the Fish an' Game Commission about that cat picture you took. They tell me it isn't a Canada lynx, but what they call a bay lynx, a bit smaller. In summer the bay lynx has a tinge of red or reddish buff in his coat. This one had probably started turning gray, like they do in cold weather. The Latin name is *Lynx rufus,* but everybody calls it a bobcat 'round here."

Skip thanked him for the information. In a way he was a little disappointed, but actually a bay lynx wasn't a bad addition to his list. He could hardly expect to find animals that all the authorities said were extinct in the area.

*   *   *

Almost before he knew it, it was November. The rain had chased away the warm days of Indian summer, and now the temperature was below freezing nearly every morning. Skip spent his spare time polishing up the reports on his project and mounting his photographs in a neat scrapbook. It made an impressive display when he finished, but there were still a number of blank pages at the end. Skip was serious about adding still more animals, though his friends and even his parents scoffed at the idea. Only Uncle Andy, who came up for a weekend, was encouraging.

"If you're going to do something like this," he told his nephew, "do it the very best you can. What you've got here is good, and I'm really impressed, but if you stop now, you can't be sure you've got a complete list of all the wild animals in Hickory County."

"I thought I might be able to find some tracks after the snow comes," said Skip. "But there doesn't seem to be much else to do right now."

"Oh, I don't know," Uncle Andy replied. "When I was a kid, I used to trap muskrats in the marsh along the Blacksnake. You don't have a muskrat yet, but I bet they're still there, and they won't go into winter quarters before the ice gets solid. Why don't we go and take a look?"

Skip was delighted. He put on old clothes and at his uncle's suggestion took along a pair of high rubber boots. They took the Retina camera and set out in the old Ford right after lunch. By that time the temperature had climbed to the upper forties. There was little traffic on the Creek Road.

"As I recall it," said Uncle Andy, "the best place to go in is right along here. Let's park the car and see what we can find."

A warm sun was shining and a few birds were chirping in the bare branches as they went through a fringe of woods.

"Easy now," Uncle Andy warned. "They've got sharp ears. If we don't make any noise, we might surprise one swimming."

Chapter Ten

They picked their way with care, trying not to step on dry twigs. Soon the woods thinned out, and they were in a brush-covered swampy area that bordered the creek. Skip held the camera ready with the zoom lens attached. He had already put on the high boots.

Suddenly his uncle nudged his arm and pointed, but all he could see was what appeared to be an irregular heap of sticks on the farther side of the stream. It was in the water, perhaps a dozen feet from the bank.

"Muskrat house," whispered Uncle Andy. "Don't move. Maybe he'll come out."

For a long time they stood perfectly still. Skip was beginning to get restless when at last he saw something move. It was a dark head, moving upstream toward the pile of twigs and brush, leaving an arrow-like wake behind. The boy lifted the camera, took a careful sight, and clicked the shutter. At once the swimming animal dove and disappeared, but he was sure he had gotten the shot.

"Good!" said his uncle. "It would be fine to get a muskrat out on the bank, where you could photograph his whole body, but this picture ought to do. You had the house in it, too, didn't you?"

Skip nodded. "The house was good and clear at the left," he said, "an' the rat was only a yard or so away from it. With the zoom lens, he ought to show up pretty well."

They waited a few minutes, but the wary animal failed to

reappear. Skip waded forward a short distance, his boots squelching in the muck, until he reached the willow-bordered bank. There was a good-sized hole there, under a root, and he was sure it had been made by one of the muskrats, but there was no sign of recent use. He took a picture of it, then returned to his uncle's side.

"Ever been up to the headwaters of the creek?" the older man asked.

"No," Skip told him. "Only a couple of miles. That place where the Hunt boys killed the coon is about as far as I've been."

"It might pay you to try it some time. The creek flows under a bridge about four miles up. Beyond that, it isn't much of a stream, but it starts somewhere on the north side of the mountain and comes down through some pretty wild country. I doubt if you could get in with a car. You'd have to hike it. I'd enjoy going, too, if I had the time and was dressed for it, but I've got to start back to Philadelphia pretty soon."

On the following weekend, Skip planned to explore the area his uncle had suggested. In the meantime, the first light snow had fallen, and the weather had turned colder again. He saw Penny at school and told her what he planned to do.

"Please, Skip," she begged, "let me come along! You know I'm a good hiker, and I wouldn't hold you back. Maybe we'll find something as exciting as the otter!"

He was a bit dubious—but still it would be fun to have some company. "You'll have to wear warm clothes," he warned. "By Saturday we might even get another snowstorm. The deer season's still a week away, so at least we don't need to worry about getting shot. But I'm going to wear a red hunting cap anyhow. With that hair of yours, you don't need one!"

"You beast!" she shot back. "My hair isn't *that* red. I've been told by nicer men than you that it's golden. Anyway,

I'll be ready bright and early Saturday. If you say you're sorry, I might even bring along something to eat."

He apologized promptly, for he knew that any food Penny brought would be delicious. After that, he watched the weather anxiously till the end of the week. Saturday morning dawned gray and cold and overcast, but the radio prediction said nothing about any expected snowfall. Skip put on his warmest clothes and, just to be on the safe side, packed a couple of old army blankets in the car. At the last moment he added an ax, thinking it might be needed for clearing the trail. As soon as he finished breakfast, he set off for the Baker house.

Penny's face was aglow when she came out the door. He was glad to see she was wearing warm ski pants and a red plaid jacket. On her bright head was a white knitted skating cap.

"Here!" she cried cheerfully. "Supplies for the expedition!" And she passed a well-filled basket into the car.

"All right," she said, jumping in beside him. "Let's go!"

They drove northward up the Creek Road for some four miles and came to the bridge where the highway crossed the stream. There Skip parked, a few yards south of the little span.

"I guess it won't make much difference which side we go up," he said, "but it's sure to be pretty rough going. Here, Penny, you carry one blanket and the ax. I'll bring the basket of grub and the other blanket."

She laughed. "Blankets? You might think we were expecting to spend the night!"

"No," he replied. "I brought 'em just in case it gets too cold. Be a good girl now and follow orders."

"Aye, aye, sir!" She chuckled and gave him a mock salute. "Lead on, captain."

The first half mile of their journey was easy. They followed a cowpath along the south side of the creek, through fairly open pasture land. Then they came to a fence, and beyond it there was nothing but forest.

"Better stay close to the creek," Skip told Penny. "That way we're in no danger of getting lost."

A few minutes later they were fighting their way through a jungle of rhododendron that grew at the bottom of a ravine. On their right, the water of the stream gurgled merrily over the stones. On their left, the ground went up in a bluff so steep that it looked unclimbable. Grimly Skip hacked away at the tough rhododendron stems with the ax. He was sure the traveling would be easier once they got beyond the ravine. Penny laughed at him.

"Maybe we'd have done better up above," she said. "Down here by the creek, it takes about ten minutes to go a hundred feet."

"O.K.," he said, panting. "Next time we'll know how to do it."

Another twenty minutes brought them out of the tangle, and they found they could move faster along a series of broad granite ledges.

"This would be a good place for a picnic," said Skip. "Only trouble is it isn't ten o'clock yet. Let's see what's up ahead."

The stream turned and twisted like a snake. Sometimes their way along the bank lay south, toward the mountain, and a few minutes later they were heading due north. Often the creek itself was hidden by thick huckleberry and alder brush that crowded the bank. There was no trail here. Their progress had to be made over and around fallen trees and through dense thickets.

Skip wondered how long Penny could take it, but she kept at his heels and made no complaint. Finally it was he himself who stopped to rest.

94

"How far do you suppose we've come?" the girl asked. "It seems like miles and miles, but I guess it can't be."

"I'd say at least two miles since we left the car," he replied. "It's taken us a couple of hours, though. Sure is wild country back here. The land may belong to some farmer, but I bet he's never followed the creek to see what it's like."

Penny shivered. "Let's keep moving," she said. "It's dark and chilly in here, and the wind's started to blow. Hear it in the pines?"

He, too, had noticed a change in the air. It was colder than when they started, and the wind seemed to be coming out of the north. Doggedly they struggled on for another mile.

"Look," said Skip. "This basket's getting heavier every step. How about it—are you ready to eat?"

"I g-guess so," she answered through chattering teeth. "But let's find a warmer place to sit down."

Skip looked at her pinched face and realized how cold she was.

"Here," he said. "I'm sorry, Penny. Come on down close to the creek, and I'll wrap that blanket around you."

They stumbled a few steps down the slope and reached a flat-topped ledge under an overhanging hemlock. The bed of the creek was a few feet below. Skip made Penny sit down on one blanket and put the other around her shoulders. Then, quickly, he went back into the woods and brought dry sticks and dead limbs for a fire. As soon as it was blazing, he opened up the lunch basket.

Besides the sandwiches, deviled eggs, and apple turnovers, Penny had packed a battered old coffeepot, instant coffee, two tin cups, and a can of sweetened condensed milk. Skip climbed down to the stream and filled the coffeepot with water. Within five minutes it was heating rapidly in the edge of a good fire.

"Funny thing," he told Penny, just to take her thoughts

off the cold. "There's only a little trickle of water coming down. You'd expect it to be quite a stream with all the rain we've had."

She had begun to feel more comfortable. "That *is* queer," she said. "Do you think we've come all the way to the beginning of the creek?"

He fed more sticks to the fire and shook his head. "No," he answered. "You can see where the stream has run full and left mud and driftwood. It must have been at least twenty feet wide a few months ago."

The coffee warmed and cheered them, and they enjoyed every mouthful of their lunch. When the last turnover was eaten, Skip got up.

"You stay here by the fire and keep warm," he told Penny. "I'd like to go up just a little farther before we turn back."

"I'm not a hothouse plant!" She laughed. "Anywhere you go, I can go. But I'm keeping the blanket around me. Let's start!"

He took the ax and the camera and led the way upstream. In a few minutes they came around a bend and saw that the ground ahead of them was swampy, with brush and undergrowth hiding whatever water there might be.

"Looks discouraging, doesn't it?" said Skip. "I reckon we'll have to chop our way again."

"Wait!" she answered, and her voice sounded excited. "Am I seeing things, or is that some kind of dam up above?"

Where she pointed, he saw a rough tangle of logs and sticks across the creek bed. It was less than a hundred yards away but difficult to see through the thickets. With no hesitation he plunged ahead.

"Penny," he said, panting, "if that's what I think it is, we've got a real find!"

They clambered over fallen logs and cut their way through tangled brush until they came near enough for a good look. Skip stared a moment, then bent over suddenly and straightened up with a piece of wood in his hand. It was as thick as his arm and about two feet long. But what thrilled them both was the way it had been cut—not hacked off with an ax or a hatchet but gnawed to a point by huge, chisel-like teeth.

"Beaver?" Penny whispered, and Skip nodded.

"Come on," he said. "We've got to see that dam close up!"

Not until they actually reached it could they appreciate how solid it was. Under the loose-looking sticks and logs was a foundation plastered with mud. Only a thin trickle of water was coming through. And above the dam a good-sized pond spread out into the surrounding thickets.

"That's why the creek was so low, down there where we ate," said Skip. "They must have just finished the dam in the last few weeks. Look at all the gnawed-off stumps around the pond—still white and fresh. And I'll bet anything that big round hump over there is a beaver house!"

He took five or six pictures of the dam, the pond, and the lodge, as well as close-ups showing the tooth marks on the cut log. The wood, he thought, was poplar, like many of the trees around the pond, and he knew that poplar bark was one of the foods that beavers like best.

"If we waited," asked Penny, "do you suppose we could see one swimming?"

But Skip thought not. It was too cold, he told her. Already there was a thin skim of ice on the edges of the pond, and the animals were probably hibernating in their lodges. Reluctantly he turned to start back, and at that moment a chill flake of snow landed on his nose. Looking up, he saw the sky full of flying white particles.

"Come on, Penny," he urged. "We'd better get out of here."

The wind was an icy blast as they struggled back through the brush. They had almost reached the ledge where the ashes of their fire lay when Penny uttered a little cry. Skip whirled to see her lying on her side, one leg crumpled under her.

"I—I turned my ankle," she gasped. "Help me up and see if I can walk."

It was no use. When she tried to stand, the ankle gave way, and she slumped to her knees again. "Darn!" she cried in exasperation. "What a stupid thing to do!"

Skip carried her to the hemlock tree and made her as comfortable as he could with the two blankets. Then he rebuilt the fire, bringing in a big pile of wood so that he could keep it going.

When the sticks were blazing and spitting in the snow, he unlaced Penny's boot and looked at her ankle. Already it was swollen to nearly twice its natural size. She had a bad sprain, and he knew they were in trouble.

"Don't worry now, Penny," he told her, trying to sound reassuring. "There's plenty of firewood, an' we can keep warm. Did you tell anybody at home where we were going?"

"Not exactly," she said miserably. "I wasn't sure, so I just said we wanted to explore the Blacksnake."

"Well," he answered, "as soon as they get worried, they're sure to find my car. And almost anybody could follow the trail we left. Here, let me rub that ankle with snow. That ought to be as good as a cold compress."

Though Penny winced with pain, she made no complaint. He thought the swelling had gone down a little when he pulled her heavy sock up over it and replaced the boot.

"Now," he said, "I'm going to heat up water and make some more coffee. It's a good thing we didn't use it all."

While the water was coming to a boil, he went up the hill behind the ledge to gather more wood. He had collected an armful of dead limbs and was just starting back when he heard a twig snap somewhere above him on the mountainside. For a fleeting instant he caught a glimpse of a man's figure—tall and shrouded in gray by the driving snow. Then the shadow was gone.

"Hey!" Skip yelled at the top of his lungs. "We need help!"

But there was no answer.

Chapter Eleven

The boy shivered with something more than the cold. He
was certain the man he had seen was the mysterious poacher
who had crossed his path before. Surely no ordinary farmer
or woodsman would have refused to answer a call for help. A
kind of hatred filled him now. He carried the wood down to
the ledge and faced Penny, hard-eyed.

"I heard you shout," she said. "Was there somebody up
there?"

"Yes," Skip answered. "The same low-down skunk that
traps otters an' snares rabbits an' won't lend a hand when
somebody's hurt. All I got was a quick look at him before he
took off. Here's your coffee. Will you be all right here? I'd
like to go up an' see if he left any tracks."

"Go ahead," she told him stoutly. "Come back soon,
though."

He bent his head into the storm and went up the slope to
the place where he had sighted the stranger. A dozen yards of
stiff climbing brought him to the top of another ledge,
where an inch of fine, granular snow had collected. And
there, headed along the ledge, he saw the prints of moccasins. They were the same big tracks he remembered from
his earlier encounter. Now, for the first time, he had a
chance to note the long strides taken by the man who wore
them. He must be long-legged and tall—over six feet, Skip
was sure.

At the western end of the ledge, the trail disappeared in a

balsam thicket. Skip thought he could have found it again on the other side, but he didn't like to leave Penny alone too long. When he returned, he found she had moved over to the fire, crawling on her hands and knees, and was putting more wood on the sputtering blaze.

Sternly he helped her back to the hemlock, where the thick, bushy branches gave some shelter from the snow.

"You've got to stay put," he told her, "an' keep those blankets around you. I'll keep the fire going."

"Did you find any tracks?" she asked.

"Yes—same moccasins as before. I figure he must be pretty tall, because he takes long steps."

"Skip," she said, after a pause, "we've got to get help up here. Why don't you go down to your car and bring somebody? I'd be fine here till you got back."

He shook his head. "I wouldn't feel right, going off and leaving you."

"Now be sensible, Skip! We can't stay here all night in this snow—why, it might turn into a regular blizzard! If I could hobble, somehow, I'd go with you."

Her words gave him new cause for thought. In another hour or two, it would be getting too dark to find the way. And every moment added to the depth of the snow. Hastily he picked up the ax and ran down to the creek bed. When he came back, he had cut a stout sapling, about four feet long, with a fork at one end. Now, with his knife, he trimmed and rounded the ends of the forking branches.

"Ever use a crutch?" he asked.

"Yes, I had to once, when I was a kid. Let me try it."

She attempted to get up at once, but he caught her arm and steadied her while she got the fork under her shoulder.

"Easy now," he urged. "It's a long way back to the car and pretty rough going. We'll stop and rest when you get tired."

He put the coffeepot and cups in the basket, picked up the ax, and led the way eastward. Penny had the two blankets draped over her shoulders Indian-fashion. She hopped along gamely on her crutch, but her progress was painfully slow.

Skip tried to pick the easiest path for her. The places where he had chopped a trail through the brush were still poor going, for stubs and limbs caught at their clothes, and more than once one of them knocked the crutch from under her arm. He looked at his watch. It was after three-thirty, and because of the storm, there would be little daylight left.

"Penny," he told her, "I'm sorry, but this just isn't going to work. I think I can make better time carrying you piggy-back if you'll let me. Come on—let's try it."

She managed a grin. "Gosh, Skip," she said, "I've sure fouled up your expedition, haven't I?"

He crouched down, and she wound her arms about his neck. She was slender enough, but dressed as she was, her muscular body must have weighed at least 120 pounds. With a heave, Skip straightened his knees and settled her on his back. Once he had a firm grip with his arms around her legs, the burden didn't seem so heavy.

"Got to leave the basket here," he grunted. "But we might need the ax. Here—you hold it across my chest. It'll give you something to hang onto."

He started out sturdily enough and made close to half a mile before he had to rest. There was a fallen tree trunk on which he deposited Penny while he stretched his tired muscles. Not far ahead, he knew, was the rhododendron jungle in the ravine, and this time he meant to avoid it if he could.

When he picked her up again, he started angling up the slope to higher ground. The climb made him breathe hard, but as he advanced, the woods seemed more open. The main trouble now was that the blowing snow had filled in the hollows. He was afraid of stepping into a crevice or tripping over a root. So he went slowly, feeling for solid ground before he put weight on his feet. They ached with the cold. He

knew Penny's must be just as painful, but he had no breath to ask her.

Now he realized he was on some kind of beaten path that led eastward along the mountainside—a deer trail perhaps. But whatever it was, it made his task easier.

"How much farther, Skip?" came Penny's voice, close to his ear. "My legs are asleep—feel as if they were about to drop off."

He struggled on a few steps to another fallen log and set her down once more. She sat there rubbing and pounding her legs with mittened fists while he straightened his stiff back and thrashed his arms.

"I bet we won't forget this for a long time," he panted, grinning at her.

"That's a sure bet," she answered. "But right now I'm scared, Skip. And the folks at home haven't even begun to worry about us yet!"

"No need to be afraid," he told her soberly. "We'll make it. Only about a mile more to go, I reckon." And he hoped he sounded surer than he felt.

Some grim possibilities had crossed his mind. If he should fall and cripple himself, or if the path they were on led nowhere and they got lost, there was a fair chance they both might freeze.

"Well," he said, "got to get this show on the road! Can you hang on for another stretch?"

"I'm ready," she told him, and again he was stumbling on under his load. He stuck to it doggedly, uphill and down, his head bowed and his eyes on the trail. In that position he could see only what lay immediately before him. It was Penny who had a better view forward.

"Skip!" she cried suddenly. "The woods are thinning out! It looks like a field or an open pasture ahead!"

Standing a little straighter and blinking through the snow, he saw that she was right. The path bore off southward through the forest, but not more than fifty yards to the east of where they stood, he could make out the rails of a fence. The sight put new heart in him.

"Hang on," he croaked. "Here we go again."

Below them, as they reached the fence, there was pasture land, dotted with scrub pines and junipers and crisscrossed by cowpaths. And beyond, they could dimly see the distant ribbon of the road.

The snow was four or five inches deep now, and Skip had to work his way down the slope with care. Once he slipped, and they both landed on their backs in a drift. Penny laughed so hard that it made her weep, and he was afraid for a minute she was hysterical. Then she wiped her eyes with a mitten and sat up.

"Poor Skip!" she said. "I'm not just an awful load to carry but a giggling one besides. Why don't you leave me right here and go to town for a stretcher and some men?"

"Don't be an idiot!" he growled. "I can carry you fine the rest of the way."

Doggedly he made it down through the pasture and staggered along the road a short distance to the car. The little old Ford stood where they had left it, forlorn under a canopy of snow. Skip got the door open and bundled Penny in. For a moment the starter ground away with no response, and his heart sank. Then, just as he was thinking this would be the last straw, the engine fired up with a roar.

When they reached Penny's house, she insisted on walking, leaning on his arm as they climbed the steps.

"Well!" Mrs. Baker hailed them cheerfully. "I was just commencing to get uneasy, with the snow and all. What's the matter, girl? You're limping!"

"That's right, Mother," Penny answered. "I sprained my ankle, like a dope. Skip had to lug me on his back most of the way home. He's probably in worse shape than I am. Do you s'pose Doc Atchison could come and look us over?"

While her mother was telephoning, Skip began to feel a little better. Never in his life had he been so close to the edge of exhaustion, but the warm, friendly room brought back some of his strength.

"Boy!" he groaned. "Am I going to be stiff tomorrow!"

Penny leaned over and patted his arm. "You were wonderful," she whispered. "I won't tell it around town, but I know you just about saved my life."

*　　*　　*

It was two hours later when Skip had changed, taken a hot shower, and eaten his supper, that he began to think about the man in the woods. At last he had actually seen him. Yet he knew no more about who he was or what he was doing on the mountain than he had guessed before.

Saturday night was always a busy time at the drugstore, and Skip went down of his own accord to see if he could help his father. By ten-thirty the young people had gone home, and the fountain business was over. Mr. Rollins replaced a few items that had been taken from the shelves, straightened up the prescription counter, and put on his coat.

"O.K., son," he said with a yawn. "Time to lock up, I guess."

They walked home together through the snowy streets. Skip had already described the beaver dam and mentioned Penny's accident. Now he brought up the subject of the poacher.

"Probably a farmer or a hired hand," his father conjectured. "Likes to roam around in the woods and isn't above taking some fur or some rabbit meat for a stew."

"That's all right except for a couple of things," Skip replied. "Why did he spoil my camera set that first time? And what kind of farmhand would it be who wouldn't try to help when a girl was hurt?"

Mr. Rollins laughed. "You've got me there," he said. "But

if he's really hiding, you don't need to worry. He can't stay hid long when a couple of hundred deer hunters start combing the woods next week."

"Well, I hope you're right, Dad, but I'm going to phone the game warden anyhow."

He put the call through as soon as he reached home, and Tom Blake sounded interested. "So you really got a look at him," he said. "Think you could identify him?"

"I doubt it," Skip told him regretfully. "He didn't give me a sight of his face, an' it was snowing hard up there. But I'd say he's a tall man—about six-two an' sort of stooped. The clothes he had on looked gray. By the way, Mr. Blake, did you know about the beaver dam?"

"What—beaver? You don't say!"

"That's right. It's over in the swampy country north of Big Hickory Mountain, on Blacksnake Creek. Looks fairly new, but beaver built it, all right. I took pictures of the dam an' one of their houses. An' there were lots of poplar trees gnawed down."

"Well, I'll be! Hasn't been a beaver colony in the county since I was a kid! I don't get over there often. How far is it?"

"Less'n three miles up the creek from the bridge. You could probably follow the trail I made."

Skip crawled into bed at eleven, aching in every muscle. His mother had guessed how tired he was, and she let him sleep late the next morning. When he finally woke, the family had gone to church, but there was orange juice in the refrigerator and eggs and bacon ready to put in the pan. For all his stiffness, he had no trouble eating a good breakfast. Then he hurried down to the darkroom to develop his film.

Penny called up later in the day. She told him the doctor had found no bones broken—just a bad sprain—and she expected to be back in school by Wednesday. Then she asked about the pictures.

"I can't tell much from the negatives," he said. "The

muskrat shot I took when I was with Uncle Andy looks like an animal swimming, that's all. But of course the muskrat lodge shows up pretty well. The beaver pictures look just fair, I guess, because the light was bad. Just the same, no other animal could have cut those trees, and the close-ups I took show every tooth mark. Tom Blake sounded pretty excited when I told him."

"I should think he might!" Penny exclaimed. "You know what you ought to do? Write an article about it for the *Welbyville Clarion*!"

"Wait a minute, now," he told her. "The fewer people who know about our beaver pond, the less danger of having 'em scared out. You wouldn't want crowds of folks rushing up there, would you?"

"Gosh, Skip—you're right. I'm not a very smart naturalist, am I? Well, at least I hope you'll report on the beaver at the next club meeting."

"I'll do that," he said. "And get well fast, so you can be my partner in the square dance."

Chapter Twelve

The November meeting of the 4-H Club at the Grange Hall was devoted more to pleasure than to business. To Skip's disappointment, Penny wasn't there, but the other girls made their reports on canning and dressmaking projects, and a few of the boys talked about plans for the winter. When it was Skip's turn, he told them he had no color slides to show. However, he had brought his black and white enlargements. He passed around the muskrat shots, and they created only mild interest.

"Before you look at these last ones," he said, "I want to get a promise from all of you that you won't talk about them outside this room."

"What did you find—a gold mine?" Dutch Krouse asked facetiously.

"Nope. Something pretty near as rare 'round here, though. Here's the first picture. Tell me what it looks like."

There were several guesses. "Driftwood?" "A pile of brush?" "A dam some kids built?"

"It's a dam, right enough, but not built by kids. Here's a close-up shot of one log. Look at the way it's cut."

"Beaver!" cried Elmer Hunt. "You mean you found 'em close by—here in the county?"

"Yes. Penny Baker was with me. We didn't see any beaver because the pond was starting to freeze, an' they must have been denned up in their lodges. But the dam's new, and they're there, all right. See—here's a picture of the pond and a beaver house."

"Where is it?" asked Joe Lukens.

"I'll tell you, but remember what I said about a promise. We want to keep the colony here, an' if crowds of people go looking for the place, the beaver are likely to move somewhere else. We went up the Blacksnake two or three miles from the place it runs under the bridge. It's real rough country over north of the mountain, so I guess mighty few men ever get in there. Elmer, are you and your brothers going deer hunting?"

"Yeah—we plan to. But we generally head down the other way. You reckon any hunters are apt to find the dam?"

"That's what I'm afraid of. But even if they did see it, I doubt if any of those city guys would know what it was. There's one other thing I wish you'd all think about. There's a stranger up there in the woods. I think he snares rabbits and does some trapping for fur. He's left his moccasin tracks a couple of times. When Penny hurt her ankle, I saw the man himself sneaking off through the trees, an' when I yelled for help, he paid no attention. All I can tell you is he's tall and a little stoop-shouldered an' maybe has a beard. No telling how old he might be. So if any of you gunners see him or find out where he lives, let Tom Blake know. He's been lookin' for him, too."

After some fruitless discussion, Ed Jones, the club leader, asked Skip how many animals he had in his project now.

"Sixteen that I've made pictures of," Skip replied. "I'm not counting the beaver yet, but if they're still around next spring, I ought to get some good shots."

"Quite a list!" Jones chuckled. "I wouldn't have believed it was possible. But you're right about not talking to folks outside 4-H. There aren't many counties in Pennsylvania that can claim a colony of wild beaver. Now, one other thing. I think I've seen your mysterious stranger."

They all stared at him openmouthed. "Yep," he went on. "I was in a little store over at Hicks' Corners last week. That's just a wide place in the road, west of the mountain. Tall fellow with a gray beard came in an' asked for salt an' flour an' bacon. After he left, I asked Mel Hicks who he was, but he said he didn't know. Thought he must live off in the woods by himself. The old codger looked it, too. Had on a gray mackinaw, old ragged pants, an' moccasins."

"Did he pay cash for his groceries?" Skip asked.

"Oh, sure. Dug down in his jeans an' pulled out a couple of greasy dollar bills. Not a very talkative man. Soon as he got the stuff he'd bought, he walked out without saying a word. I didn't notice which way he went, but I'm certain he was afoot. There wasn't any sound of a car starting up."

Skip drew a deep breath. "It could have been him, at that," he said. "I only guessed at the beard, but I thought from the way he slouched along, he wasn't a young man. An' if he lives on game he poaches, bacon an' flour an' salt'd be about all he'd need."

Joe Lukens joined Skip at the table when the pumpkin pies were brought in. "I've been tryin' to figure where a man could hole up on Big Hickory," he said. "Maybe his hide-out isn't on the mountain at all. There's woods all 'round to the west an' north. Most of the year, of course, only a few people ever go there, but you'd think the hunters'd be sure to spot any kind of shack."

Skip nodded, his mouth full of pie. "I've thought the same thing. There are a couple of other possibilities, though. It could be the man wasn't here in deer season last year—just came since spring. Or he might live in one of the caves over on the northwest slope. That's where I saw the big rattler, you know, so I sure didn't go in to find out."

"Well," Joe said with a sigh, "in another month the snow'll be deep. I guess we'll have to wait for spring to look for him."

"Unless we had snowshoes," Skip pointed out. "I think my dad's got an old pair. Any at your house?"

"Gee, come to think of it, I believe there are some! I'll get 'em out an' see if they're any good. Then we'll both have to do some practicin' so we can use 'em."

*　　*　　*

The deer season opened with gray skies and a threat of more snow. Every motel and boardinghouse within miles of Welbyville was full by Sunday night, and late-comers kept arriving the next day, their cars churning through the slush of Main Street. The local doctors shook their heads and laid out their instruments. They knew from experience that there were sure to be shooting accidents.

Quite a few of the older boys were absent from school that week. It was Wednesday before Elmer Hunt showed up for classes, but he had killed his buck.

"Got a lucky shot," he told Skip. "We were in the woods early, ahead of most of the outsiders, an' my brother Lew nailed a four-pointer that first morning. Then, close to sunset, Bill took a long shot at another buck an' wounded it. We came up with the cripple just before dark an' finished it off with a knife. Yesterday I went down to the same piece of woods by myself. A feller from the city was there ahead of me, an' he started a big buck but fired wild. The deer was headed right for me, runnin' lickety-split, an' I had to take a quick aim. Got him square in the heart. He's a beauty, too— six-pointer."

"What did the city man say to that?" Skip asked.

"Oh, he put up a little argument, but I let him look at the carcass, an' he had to agree there was only one bullet hole. He'd shot from the rear, so it had to be mine."

"Congratulations," Skip told him. But inwardly he knew he could never have fired at the buck himself. He just wasn't cut out to kill things, he guessed.

"We didn't see anything of your wild man," Elmer went on. "I reckon he's keeping himself under cover this week."

Once the hunting was over, the venison hung in outdoor sheds to freeze, and the once proud heads mounted by the local taxidermist, Hickory County settled down for the long pull through winter. More snow fell, piling deep drifts in the fields and lanes. The main roads were kept open by the busy plows, but in the back country, farmers had to dig their own paths. It was a real hardship for some of the 4-H boys to get out to the school buses.

Skip asked his father about the snowshoes. They had been laid away in the attic for years, and when he saw them, he was dismayed. The frames appeared to be stout enough, but nearly all the rawhide lacing was mouse-eaten and frayed. Joe Lukens reported that his were in much the same condition.

Out at the edge of town, there was an old harness maker who still clung to his diminishing trade. The boys went to see him and found he had a couple of dusty untanned hides under a pile of harness leather. He was willing to cut them up, and for five cents a foot, he made them neat, narrow thongs of the size they needed. It took nearly ten yards of the stuff for each snowshoe, but Skip and Joe felt the six dollars they paid was cheap enough. The task of wetting, stretching, and knotting the thongs took several evenings and wasn't finished until the day before Thanksgiving.

"What do you say, Joe?" Skip suggested. "Want to try some snowshoeing Friday on the mountain—if the weather's good, that is?"

"Sure. I'll practice a little an' get the hang of it. I'd rather go on skis, but there aren't any open slopes up there."

"Snowshoes aren't hard to handle," Skip assured him. "I was out on mine for half an hour this morning."

His confidence may have been a little premature. Another four inches of light snow fell that night, and on Thanksgiving morning he decided to work up an appetite for dinner. Putting on the snowshoes, he went rapidly up past the cornfield and into the woods above. He found his progress was fine where there was a path. After that, he kept getting the frames tangled up in brush and brambles.

There must be a trick to it, he thought, and after a few more mishaps, he discovered what it was. If he lifted his forward foot high, with the toe slanting upward, it came down on top of the twigs or vines and simply trod them into the snow.

By noon he had covered two or three miles, and his thighs ached from the unaccustomed strain. Once back in his room, he changed his clothes and rubbed the sore muscles with liniment. When he came limping down to dinner, his father was chuckling.

"How do you like snowshoeing, son?" he asked. "Easy as you thought it would be?"

"I'm beginning to learn the tricks," Skip answered stubbornly. "It sure teaches you about muscles you never knew you had, though."

At that moment they heard the sound of a horn outside, and when Skip hurried to the door, he was happy to see his uncle's sports car in the driveway.

"Gee, Uncle Andy!" he cried. "Nobody told me you'd be here!"

"Couldn't keep me away," said the older man with a grin. "I've been smelling roast turkey and mince pie all the way up."

They were a merry group at dinner, and when they finally rose, full almost to bursting, Skip hastened to show his uncle the newest additions to his collection of animal pictures.

"Did you guess," he asked, "what we'd find up at the headwaters of Blacksnake Creek? Remember, it was you who told me I ought to take a trip up there."

"Well, it was a sort of hopeful hunch. When I was a little

shaver, I explored a bit with my dad. We found an old broken dam and some gnawed logs that must have been there a long time. The beaver had left, probably years before, but I knew they sometimes come back."

"They're back now, all right," Skip told him. "These shots prove it, and when the ice goes out in the spring, I'm hoping to get more pictures—of live, working beaver."

Uncle Andy nodded. "That's fine," he said. "You know, I've been thinking about this project of yours. There are two or three magazines that specialize in animal photographs— not just the hunting and sports magazines, but some that are devoted to wildlife conservation. There's no need to do anything yet, but some day I'd like to see your story about the animals of a single county published in one of them. Maybe I could give you some help with the writing part."

"Gosh!" That was all Skip could say for a minute. The idea seemed too improbable for him to take it in at first, but he soon found his tongue again.

"You really think somebody would buy it? Maybe the pictures aren't too bad, but I'm not much of a writer. Still, I'd sure like to try if you'll give me some advice!"

That night Skip took a fresh look at his photographs, trying to imagine how they might appear in the pages of a magazine. There were five or six that he was sure would reproduce well. The color pictures would probably have to be left out, for he knew that full-color plates were pretty expensive.

Before he went to bed, he looked outside and saw more snow was falling. He hoped it would clear by daybreak, for he and Joe had planned to go up on the mountain.

The storm was still blowing strong when he woke Friday morning. He got Joe on the phone, and they agreed to postpone the expedition at least a day. Then Skip went out with the shovel to dig paths and clear the driveway, for eight or nine inches of snow had already fallen, and where the wind had a sweep, the drifts were above his knees. By the time he finished, the clouds were breaking to show a few patches of blue in the northwest—a sure sign of clearing weather.

Skip and his uncle discussed the possibility of taking some winter pictures that day. "In deep snow like this," Uncle Andy said, "all the smaller animals will be denned up. Only the snowshoe rabbits would be out, and they're white, so they'd hardly show on your camera. Still, I suppose a fox or a bobcat might try to trail one. Don't be too disappointed if you find you can't get any pictures tomorrow."

"I wish we had another set of snowshoes," Skip told him. "It would be more fun if you could go along."

His uncle laughed. "I'm afraid I'm not in practice," he said. "That kind of exercise would probably lame me up for a week."

Saturday came in clear and cold, and by nine o'clock Skip was ready to start. He took along some lunch and reached Joe Lukens' place by nine-thirty. The plows had been out, and all the main roads were cleared. Because of its weight, Skip had left the Graflex at home and carried only the smaller camera.

"Hi!" Joe yelled from the back door. "Be with you in a second. I'm takin' along some grub to cook, if we can find a place to build a fire."

"O.K.," Skip answered. "But you'd better bring a couple of sandwiches too—just in case. I've got a feeling we'll find a lot of deep snow up in the woods."

Chapter Thirteen

The temperature hung close to the zero mark that morning. Skip drove carefully, following the cleared road up over the shoulder of Big Hickory. The worst trouble they encountered was finding a place to park, for the plow had banked the snow high along the narrow track. At last they reached a place where the wind had swept a clear spot on the shoulder, so they left the car there and put on their snowshoes.

They weren't too far from the old lumber trail where Skip had gone into the woods on earlier occasions. It was covered deep in snow now, but once they had located the entrance, it was easier to follow than trying to plow through brush and timber.

"Right about here," Joe said, "was where you set up your camera on the deer trail, wasn't it—an' then found the trap sprung? I wonder where your mystery man is now. Shouldn't think it'd be much fun livin' in the woods in weather like this!"

Skip, who was leading the way, went on a few steps before he answered. Then he halted so suddenly that Joe almost ran into him.

"You wanted to know where he is," Skip whispered. "Well, I can tell you—look at that."

He was pointing to a line of big, nearly circular depressions in the snow. They were only about three inches deep and must have been made after the storm ended, for their outlines were sharp.

"Bear-paw snowshoes!" Skip exclaimed. "They didn't come in from the road or we'd have seen 'em. He's headed the same way we are—see how the snow's sprayed up along the rear edges?"

"Golly!" Joe murmured, bending for a closer look. "Maybe he's only a little way ahead. You goin' to follow him?"

"I sure am," Skip replied. "It's the best chance I've had to find out who he is an' what he does up here. You're game, aren't you?"

"Yeah." Joe hesitated. "I'll come along. But I'd feel better if I'd brought a gun."

Skip chuckled. "I doubt if you need one. This fellow's queer, but I somehow don't believe he's dangerous. What I'd like to do is sneak up on him an' get a picture."

The snowshoe trail led over a spur of the mountain's shoulder and down into the woods, close to the place where Skip had once found himself in the swamp. The boys watched for animal tracks as they went. As Uncle Andy had warned, the snow was too deep for most small creatures, but Skip did come on the furry trail of a snowshoe rabbit. It had been taking short hops and sinking an inch or two through the surface. They were surprised, a moment later, to find a deep, broad depression where the rabbit's tracks stopped. At its edges were the marks of huge wings, and a single spot of blood remained to mark the rabbit's death.

"Must have been a mighty big owl," Skip whispered. "A great horned owl, I reckon—or even a snowy. They come this far south in the middle o' winter."

The light fell on the depression in such a way that there were interesting blue shadows, and the fleck of blood stood out sharply. Skip stopped long enough to make a close-up color shot, then picked up the trail of the bear-paw snowshoes once more.

It skirted the edge of the swamp, bearing to the west, then

disappeared into what looked like an impenetrable hemlock thicket. The boys paused there and held a whispered consultation.

"He could be layin' for us in there," Joe warned. "If he spotted us comin', he probably ducked into the brush to wait."

Skip shook his head. "I don't think so," he whispered. "It's just as likely he lives back in there, an' if that's it, I want to see his house. You stay here if you'd rather."

He didn't wait to see if Joe followed him but crouched low and plunged into the thicket. The man on the bear-paw snowshoes who had preceded him had knocked most of the loose snow off the hemlock boughs, but cold bits of it still fell on his neck. He clutched the camera, shielding it inside his mackinaw, and with his other hand pushed aside the brush. It was hard to see just where he was going, but the tracks continued to lead forward.

After ten yards or so, he could see a thinning of the branches ahead. He stopped, looking and listening, and to his astonishment he heard a loud snort close by. Cautiously he leaned forward and peered in the direction from which the sound had come. Something moved there. He saw the antlered head of a buck, then the big ears and startled eyes of two does. They were all below the level of the surrounding snow, so that only their heads and necks were visible. He realized then that he had come upon a "yard," trampled out by the deer to give them forage in the deep snow. He had heard vaguely of such a thing, but only a few old hunters had actually seen a deer yard.

For the moment Skip forgot all about the stranger whose trail he had been following. He took a careful step or two so that the camera lens would be unobstructed, adjusted the focus, checked on the scene in the viewfinder, and clicked the shutter.

At the sound the buck snorted again. Then another animal lumbered to its feet among the deer—something bigger than they were, and black and white in color. It was a cow!

Grinning, Skip started to take another picture and was just in the act of pressing the button when he heard a yell from Joe.

"Hey!" the boy was shouting. "Look—there he goes!"

Skip swung hastily about, but Joe's voice had come from beyond the thicket, and he could see nothing in that direction. He stooped again and forced his way back through the hemlock brush. When he emerged, panting, his friend had started off up the slope in pursuit of the elusive stranger. Skip caught a glimpse of Joe's red plaid jacket and hurried to catch up. He finally overtook the other boy at the foot of a high ledge, part way up the mountainside.

"I saw him plain," Joe gasped. "He came out of those hemlocks off to the right of where you went in. But he sure can move when he wants to. I lost sight of him quite a ways back."

"What became of his tracks?" Skip asked. "Weren't you trailing him?"

"Sure—this far. But now I can't find 'em. Do you see any sign of where he went?"

Skip looked around him at the surface of the snow, unbroken by any tracks except their own. It was uncanny, but the trail had completely disappeared.

"What was he like?" he asked Joe. "You said you got a good look at him."

"Tall—stooped over a little—an' his beard was long an' pretty near white. He had on a gray jacket an' a sort of a mangy-lookin' fur cap. He sure did travel fast on those round snowshoes, though!"

Skip nodded. "Same fellow I saw," he said. "I'm beginning to think he's just too smart for us. Doggone it—his trail must go *somewhere!* He couldn't just vanish in the air."

Slowly they circled, like hounds casting for a scent. The

round tracks were there, all right. But they came straight up to the foot of the cliff and stopped. It was some minutes before Skip remembered to tell his companion about the deer yard in the thicket.

"There was a buck an' two does in there," he said. "The old man must have known just where they were when he went in through that brush. Maybe he was all set to kill one. Did he have a gun?"

"Not that I could see," Joe replied. "No—I'm sure he didn't. He was swingin' his arms when he ran, an' there was no gun."

"One other thing," said Skip. "Believe it or not, there was a black an' white cow in the yard with the deer! Any idea who she might belong to?"

Joe stared, unbelieving. "A cow!" he exclaimed. "You're kidding! I did hear the Krouses lost a Holstein heifer back last spring, though. They figured she'd been stolen, but Pa said it was more likely she'd busted through the fence an' just wandered off."

Skip nodded. "That sounds reasonable. She's probably been living wild in the woods, an' when the deep snow caught her, she was lucky to be with the deer."

The mystery of how the man on the bear-paw webs had vanished was still unsettled. The tracks were there, half obliterated by their own, and yet up near the ledge they were gone. The boys puzzled over it for a while, then decided it was time to eat their sandwiches. The sun had gone behind clouds, and it was very cold.

Skip found an open space at the foot of the cliff where he knew it would be safe to build a fire. He set off to find some dry wood and finally located a dead pine lying in the snow. He had no ax, but some of the dry limbs broke off readily. For kindling, he cut a handful of shavings with his knife. Meanwhile, Joe had been using one of his snowshoes as a shovel to dig away the snow from the face of the rock. As

Skip returned, the other boy straightened up and thrashed his arms.

"Hurry up an' get it lighted," he urged. "I'm 'most frozen stiff."

Skip laid his wood carefully, put the shavings underneath, and lit a match. Sheltering the flame with his hand, he was cheered to see an edge of the tinder begin to burn. Slowly the blaze increased, licking upward to the dry wood. And just at that instant a mass of snow tumbled down from the top of the ledge, smothering the fire completely.

"Aw, heck!" said Joe in disgust. "What in thunder made that happen?"

Skip was wondering himself. He looked up at the crest of the ledge, some twenty feet above. As far as he could see, there was no overhanging drift. It seemed very strange that a pile of snow should drop in exactly the right place to ruin their little fire.

"Well," he said practically. "I guess we can make out with a cold lunch, anyhow. After that, the best way to get warm'll be to start for home."

But as he munched a sandwich, he kept on thinking about that small avalanche. It seemed like too much of a coincidence. Then his mind jumped to the gray-bearded stranger, and he gave a start. The fact that they had lost his trail didn't mean that he was far away. And dousing their fire was just the sort of trick they might expect from him.

An idea had begun to form in Skip's head. He got up and walked slowly along by the foot of the ledge. There were a number of big trees growing near, and one large hemlock had branches that stretched out over the top of the cliff. Would it be possible, he wondered, for a man with powerful arms to swing himself up into one tree, go on by way of the branches to the next, and finally crawl along the hemlock limb to land on top of the ledge? Perhaps he had been mistaken in thinking of the strange character on the mountain as a feeble old man. Even if his hair and beard were white, he had already proved he could move fast in the woods.

Skip went back to the place where the round snowshoe tracks had disappeared. Now that he looked closer, he could see the prints were deeper there, as if they had been the takeoff for a jump. And there was an overhanging branch about eight feet above the snow.

"What you lookin' for, Skip?" Joe asked through chattering teeth. "I thought you were ready to go home."

"I am," Skip told him. "Just wanted to see how our old friend managed to get away so slick. Now I think I know. Take a look at these last snowshoe tracks. See how they're sunk in, as if he'd made a jump?"

"Sure," said Joe. "But he couldn't jump more'n eight or ten feet, an' I hunted around in all directions to see where he landed."

"Not *all* directions!" Skip chuckled. "I reckon he jumped straight up an' grabbed that limb overhead. Once he pulled himself up on it, he could slip off the snowshoes, throw 'em up on top o' the ledge, an' then work his way along from tree to tree till he got to that big hemlock. That's how he came to be waiting up on top, maybe watching us till he had a chance to push snow down on our fire."

"Gosh!" said Joe. "You're sure smart to figure that out. But you don't aim to follow him, do you? I'm so cold, I don't know as I'll ever thaw out."

Skip felt somewhat the same way. "O.K.," he replied. "I just thought maybe you'd like to get a peek at those deer an' the cow, but we'll head straight back to the car if you'd rather."

Joe hesitated, but an attack of shivering brought his decision. "Honest, Skip," he said, "I'd better take your word for the deer yard. I'm close to freezin'."

Skip led the way down the hill, forcing a pace he knew would start his friend's circulation again. By the time they reached the plowed road, Joe was too much occupied with keeping up to have any breath left for complaining. They stripped off their snowshoes, climbed in, and set off for home.

"You know," said Skip, as they drove into the Lukens' dooryard, "I don't believe that old man is as mean as we'd figured. He didn't do anything to really hurt us. Maybe he just wants to scare us out, so we won't get in his way or interfere with whatever he's doing up there."

"Well," Joe replied, "far's I'm concerned, he can keep his stinkin' woods an' snow to himself."

Skip laughed. "O.K.," he said. "Unless you change your mind, I guess I'll have to take my snowshoe trips alone. You'd better hurry inside, Joe, an' get warm. You're still shaking."

He drove on home and was glad to enter the heated house. That evening he telephoned Dutch Krouse.

"Dutch," he said, "I heard you folks had lost a Holstein heifer a few months back."

"Yeah, that's right. We had her with some other young stock back in the west forty, where it's mostly woods. She was the only one missin', though. Guess she must ha' broke through the fence. Why—you seen her?"

"I think so. Joe Lukens an' I were up on the mountain today, an' I came across a deer yard. There were three deer in it, an' one black an' white cow. You won't be able to get her out for a while, though. Drifts are three or four feet deep all around the yard, an' it's close to a mile from the nearest road."

"How'd you get in if the snow was so deep?" asked Dutch suspiciously.

"Snowshoes," Skip explained. "I got a picture of the deer, an' maybe the cow shows, too. Soon as I get it developed, I'll let you see it."

"All right," said Dutch, "but you better not be kiddin'

me. My old man was real upset when the heifer turned up missin'."

"Good," Skip couldn't resist saying. "Then I guess he'll be ready to pay a nice reward."

"Him?" Dutch snorted. "You know durn well how tight he is with a nickel. But I'll tell him you think you know where she is an' see what he says."

Chapter Fourteen

The next gathering of the 4-H Club was livelier than usual for that time of year. With Christmas just ahead, the girls were full of reports on the fruitcake and cookies they had made. And there was some curiosity about the trip Skip and Joe had made in the deep snow. By luck Skip had his color transparencies back in time for the meeting, and the picture of the place where the owl had killed the rabbit was fine and clear. Even the red splotch of blood showed up so well that it caused shivers among the girls.

Then he came to the slide he had taken at the deep-trampled deer yard, and it was the boys' turn to get excited. Just visible beyond the heads of the buck and does was a small patch of black and white. Apparently the heifer had been less alert than her companions and hadn't lifted her head until after the shot.

"Of course, Dutch," Skip commented, "you couldn't tell from that whether she's the one you lost. But she's there, all right. I can take you to the place if you want to go in on snowshoes."

Krouse grunted. "No point in that if we can't get her out," he said. "I'm willin' to wait until some of the snow melts."

Skip wasn't planning to mention their glimpse of the "Old Man of the Mountain," as some of the youngsters had started to call him. But Joe Lukens was bursting to talk about it.

"He's a slick one, all right," he told them. "I got one good sight of him while Skip was takin' the picture of the deer. But he got away mighty fast, an' when we tried to trail him, his tracks just disappeared. Then a little while later, when we were tryin' to build a fire an' thaw out, durned if he didn't heave a mess of snow down an' put it out!"

They all laughed at that. "How do you know he did it?" Penny Baker asked. "Couldn't the snow have just slid down on your fire?"

Both the boys who had been there shook their heads. "I'm pretty sure it was done on purpose," said Skip reluctantly. "We sort of figured out how he got up there, too, but it would take a mighty smart, active man to do it."

He went on to describe the ledge, the trees, and the place where the bear-paw tracks had ended. "That's the only way to explain how he did his vanishing act," he concluded.

"Well, shucks!" Elmer Hunt put in. "Why didn't you climb up there an' trail him some more?"

"Maybe we should have," Skip admitted. "But by that time, Joe, here, was about half frozen. We decided we'd better get home."

"So," said Penny, "he's as much of a mystery as ever. I'm sort of glad in a way. He gives me the shivers, but it's exciting to know he's up there on the mountain."

Some of the boys were all for forming a posse, taking guns, and going after the white-bearded man. But more snow had fallen that week, and when Skip reminded them they would have to travel on snowshoes, their belligerent attitude cooled off somewhat.

"Besides," he told them, "what makes you think this fellow's a criminal? He could have stolen my camera, but he didn't. Maybe he's just a hermit that likes to be left alone in the woods. That isn't against the law."

"How about trapping that otter?" Elmer asked. "It was out of season, too."

"I've got no proof he set the trap—just a footprint we found twenty yards away. It could have been somebody else who wanted that otter skin. Anyhow, it's a matter for the game warden to settle. He knows the whole story, an' I reckon he's been doing something about it."

He took Penny home in his car, and her thoughts were still on the same subject.

"I believe you're getting almost fond of Old White-Whiskers," she said teasingly. "What's made you change?"

"Oh, I don't know," he replied. "Maybe it's because I admire his foxiness—the handy way he gets around. At least he knows the mountain better'n anybody else in the county."

"You think he'll leave our beaver colony alone?" she asked.

"That does worry me a little. But if my hunch is right, he won't bother 'em. Darn it, though, I could be awfully wrong!"

They pulled up at Penny's door, but she didn't get out at once. "Skip," she said, "I wish I could go up and see those deer in their yard. Can't you take me?"

"Look, Penny," he told her, "you know I'd like to. But you've never been on snowshoes, and it's hard work. Besides, your ankle isn't any too strong yet. You don't want me to have to carry you out again, do you? It wouldn't be easy in snow as deep as it is up there."

"You're right." She laughed. "We'd better wait till I've had a chance to practice. Good night, now!"

*　　*　　*

Skip fully intended to go back into the woods, alone if necessary, but he had no opportunity until the end of the second week in December. There had been no more storms, but because of continued cold weather, very little of the snow on the ground had melted. Day after day the temperature stayed around zero, hovering between ten below and ten above.

At last came a Saturday when he was able to get away. Dressed in his warmest clothes, he took his small camera, an ax, and a little food, and packed them along with his snowshoes in the back of the old car. Not knowing what the back roads would be like, he also carried tire chains.

He got a fairly early start. By ten o'clock he was over west of the mountain, on the road that ran north past Hicks' Corners. When he reached the little store, he parked the car and went in.

Mel Hicks, the storekeeper, was a stout man in a heavy old sweater who seemed to spend most of his time feeding wood to the sheet-iron stove. Skip warmed his hands before it and then bought a couple of candy bars as a preliminary to starting a conversation.

"A friend o' mine," he said, "a fellow named Ed Jones, from Welbyville, told me he'd seen a queer-looking old duck in here about a month ago. Said he was a tall man, sort of stooped, with a gray beard. I believe he asked you if you knew who he was. Tell me, Mr. Hicks, has the man been back to buy anything?"

Hicks shook his head. "I remember the time," he said. "Old feller bought a few staples an' left. I'd seen him once before that, but he hasn't been back since. Why—you know anything about him?"

"I've seen him a couple of times, that's all. Just a quick glimpse, up in the woods. I'd sure like to find out where he lives an' what he does for a living, though."

Again the storekeeper shook his head. "I've wondered myself," he replied. "Can't help you, I'm afraid. At a guess, he's camped somewhere up on the mountain. As long as he pays me cash money, I don't ask questions."

"Sure," said Skip. "I understand. I was just curious, that's all."

He finished munching one of the candy bars, then started the engine and rattled on up the road. Soon he reached the entrance to the rough track he had followed that Indian summer day when he had seen the rattlesnake. It was in his mind now, in the bitter weather, he might safely explore that rocky hillside where the caves were.

Even with the tire chains, he doubted if the car could make it up that trail. So he put on his snowshoes and started to climb on foot. The snow was nearly two feet deep on the rocky trail but packed hard enough so that his webs barely sank in.

The woodland looked very different from the way it had when he saw it last. Remembering how the October sun had made him sweat, he wished some of that warmth might return now. But as long as he kept climbing, he didn't mind the cold. Landmarks were difficult to recognize in their winter garb. He thought he passed the pine clump where the grouse had been drumming, and then the spot where he had photographed the fighting squirrels. Finally, as the mountainside grew steeper, he knew he was approaching the boulder-strewn slope where the big rattler had been lying in the sun.

Up above him, through the trees, he could see the granite face of the high ledge, and his heart beat a little faster, for he thought of the caves and what might be in them.

A moment later he stopped short, staring at a trail that crossed his own. The tracks weren't fresh but still fairly distinct—the oval-shaped prints of bear-paw snowshoes! Skip wasn't really surprised. He had had a feeling all along that this rocky slope might hold a clue to the old man's secret hide-out.

He waited a little to gather his courage. All the way up the hill, he had been carrying the ax in one hand and the pail of lunch in the other. His camera was slung from the strap around his neck. Now he wanted both hands free to take pictures. He put down the ax against the trunk of a tree and hung the food pail on a handy limb.

The old snowshoe trail slanted upward to the right, though he couldn't be sure which direction the wearer had been traveling. As he followed the tracks, he became surer than ever that they would lead to one of the caves. But in among the big rocks, the trail suddenly swung right again, leading off along a ridge that stretched down into the woods.

It appeared his guess had been wrong. But why had the old man come up here? Had he, too, been interested in those dark openings in the cliff, or had he merely chosen this route because it avoided the thick brush below?

Skip hesitated a moment. The trail, he thought, was at least two days old, and it would still be there if he wanted to follow it later. Meanwhile, he would never have a better chance to look into the caves. Shivering a little in the cold, he turned back and started scrambling upward among the boulders.

The first cave he came to was disappointing. It was little more than a wide crack in the face of the ledge, and so shallow that he could see the rear wall. Snow had drifted into the mouth of the aperture to a depth of several feet. The surface was undisturbed by the track of any man or animal.

He moved on, placing his snowshoes carefully, for he knew there might be deep crannies underneath the white blanket. Ten or twelve strides brought him to another cave, more promising than the first. Again he saw no tracks leading in, but the opening was wider and appeared to extend farther into the ledge. He waited to stiffen his determination, then took a deep breath and stepped forward. The entrance was so low that he had to bow his head to keep from bumping it. Almost immediately he was in semidarkness.

A few feet inside, the snow ended, and he felt the crunch of rocky fragments under his rawhide webs. Ahead of him the blackness deepened. Without a light it was impossible to tell how far the cavern reached. He had brought along some matches, thinking he might want to build a fire. Now he took off his mitten, put it in his pocket, and struck a match on the dry rock wall of the cave. Then he hurried forward, trying to get as far as he could before the flickering flame went out.

Ahead of him the chamber seemed to widen a little, but twenty feet farther in, it narrowed again and made a sharp bend to the left. The floor was fairly level, covered with scraps of stone, a few small bones, and other debris. Skip was sure that foxes, bobcats, or other animals must have used the place in the past, for the bones looked like the remains of rabbits.

He paused again at the turning to light another match. It was warmer here than it had been outside, and there was a strong, peculiar scent in the still air. After two or three whiffs of it, he lost most of his desire to explore much farther. Something, either the odor or plain cowardice, told him to get out before he found himself in trouble. He shook his shoulders impatiently, set his jaw, and took a cautious step through the narrow opening, holding the match high over his head.

At first all he could see was that this was a smaller chamber than the outer one. It was irregular in shape and hardly more than five yards long. The smell in that confined space was almost overpowering—a rank animal smell that sent a chill of fear down his spine. And just as the match flickered out, he saw a huge, black, furry shape in the farthest corner!

Skip stood there in pitchy darkness for a few heartbeats, scarcely daring to breathe. At last his shaking fingers pulled out another match, and he managed to light it, backing hastily out of the cavern. Not until he reached the lovely daylight and filled his lungs with sweet, clean air did he begin to feel safe. Even then, though he knew the bear he had seen was deep in its winter sleep, he still looked back over his shoulder. The cold air felt good after the stuffiness of the cave, and he went at a brisk pace down the hill to get his ax and lunch pail.

The ax was there, leaning against the tree just as he had left it. But the tin bucket was gone! Astonished, he looked around to see if it had fallen off the limb. Then his eye fell on an oval snowshoe print close to the tree. Had it been there before? He couldn't be sure, but certainly the pail had disappeared. On the hard, crusted snow, it was almost impossible to spot a fresh trail. If the mysterious gray-beard had stolen his lunch, he had probably gone off, planting his webs in the same tracks he had made earlier.

Skip was disgusted. If he had only thought to bring along some flash bulbs, he would at least have had an unusual picture to show for his hungry day of scouting. As it was, all he could do was tell what he had found, and the boys would promptly scoff at the idea. Penny, at least, would understand and believe him. Meanwhile, even though he now had nothing to eat, he decided to make a try at following the bear-paw snowshoe trail.

It made little difference which way the tracks were pointed. The old man must either have been coming from his dwelling place or going back to it. Skip moved westward, keeping his eye on the line of tracks and working his way through thickets of spruce and hemlock. He marveled at the stranger's ability to penetrate such places, apparently without even breaking stride.

After the better part of an hour of such going, Skip was around on the northwest shoulder, in a part of the woods he had never seen before. There the trail became confused, with tracks going off in all directions. It looked like a deliberate attempt to throw off any pursuer, and the boy grew more and more puzzled. After following two or three false trails into hopeless tangles of brush, he came back to his starting point and looked up at the sky to get his bearings. The day was no longer bright. A dark cloud bank was piling up in the north, and already a film had covered the noon sun. From the signs he knew that snow was coming. Angry and frustrated, he set off down the mountain to get back to his car.

Chapter Fifteen

It took Skip longer than he expected to find the old Ford, for the snowshoe trail had led him a long way from his starting point. As a matter of fact, he came out on the road only a short distance above Hicks' store and had to tramp back up the hill to the place where he had parked. By the time he got the car turned around and started for home, it had begun to snow, lightly at first, then in a thicker curtain of white.

Driving took most of his attention, but in the back of his mind he was still thinking about the morning's adventures. Each moment he became surer that the mysterious stranger had robbed him of his lunch. It fitted the pattern. The ax had not been touched, which must mean all the old man wanted was food. Or was he still trying to discourage Skip from exploring the mountain? Well, the boy vowed to himself that he wouldn't give up. After this storm ended, he would come back and get a flash photo of the hibernating bear, no matter what happened.

The snow was nearing blizzard proportions when he reached home. A northeast wind of increasing force blew the flakes wildly, and he was barely able to plow through the drifts to the barn. His parents had expected him to be gone all day, but he found his mother very glad to see him home. In the kitchen he thrashed his arms to shake off the chill and asked if there was anything to eat.

"Why," she said in surprise, "I thought you took some lunch!"

"I did." He laughed. "Didn't seem to stay by me, though. What I need now is something hot an' filling."

He ate the soup she warmed up for him and followed it with a big wedge of pie and a glass of milk. Then he told her about searching the cave and coming on the bear.

"I bet he's the same big bear that was busting up Joe Lukens' beehives," he said. "He was sure fast asleep, but I didn't hang around to see if I could wake him. Next time I go up there, I'll have the flash attachment on the camera and get a picture of him."

He could see the worry in her face and was glad he hadn't mentioned the theft of his lunch. She was upset enough without that. At supper he told his father about the bear's den.

"You got a good look at him?" John Rollins asked. "No question about its being a bear?"

"That's right. I had a match lit, an' I could see him plain —all curled up, but big as a house. I was sure from the rank smell, too."

"Well," said his father, "you probably weren't in any danger. When a bear goes into his winter sleep, it's really more like a coma. He doesn't wake up easy. But before you try any flash pictures, I suggest you call up the game warden. He might want to go along with you."

Skip knew that Tom Blake had been away for a week at the state capital, straightening out some matter of hunters' licenses. On the chance that he had returned, he gave the warden a call that night.

Blake's gruff voice answered. "I'd like to see this bear myself," he told Skip when he had heard his story. "I've noticed those caves an' wondered if any animals denned up there. But we can't do much about it until this storm's over. When's your school let out for Christmas vacation?"

"Not until next weekend," Skip replied. "But I guess that

old bear'll still be there. You want to give me a call when you can go?"

They agreed to make the trip the following Saturday if the weather improved and nothing else interfered. Skip wanted to talk to Blake about the mystery man but decided to wait until their expedition to the cave. It wouldn't hurt to do a little more thinking first.

The snow fell steadily all that night, but by sunrise it had stopped. In all, about another eight or ten inches had been deposited on top of the old crust. During that week a number of carloads of skiers drove up through Welbyville on their way to slopes in the Catskills and Adirondacks. Skip would have liked to join them, but the final week of school kept him busy.

Only to Penny had he confided his adventure on the mountain, and he knew she wouldn't talk to anybody else. He was afraid some trigger-happy hunter would try to kill the bear in its den if the word spread.

Another few inches of snow fell on Thursday, but the roads were plowed out next day. And on Friday night, Tom Blake phoned to say he would pick Skip up early Saturday morning. This time Skip packed the flash attachment and fresh bulbs for his camera. Also, at Mrs. Rollins's insistence, he took along enough sandwiches for both the warden and himself.

Blake had a four-wheel-drive jeep, ideal for the rough country he had to cover on his rounds. By nine o'clock they were up on the west side of Big Hickory and nearing the trail Skip had used in reaching the caves. He pointed the place out to the warden, who pulled the jeep over into the roadside snow and parked it.

"Got a good day for a hike in the woods," he told Skip, as he fastened his snowshoe straps. "Not quite as cold as it was a while back, an' nice bright sunshine."

Out of the rear of the jeep, he took a high-powered rifle. "Don't expect to use this," he said with a laugh, "but it won't hurt to have it handy. Here, you carry this flashlight in your knapsack."

It was a big five-cell torch that would throw a lot of light —much better than matches, Skip thought. Blake let him lead the way, since this was his expedition. For half an hour they plodded up the slope in silence, their webs creaking softly in the new light snow. Then, when they were well up the mountain, the warden spoke.

"Got my bearings now," he said cheerfully. "Why not let me break trail for a spell. You'll find it easier walking in my tracks."

Skip had been puffing a bit, and he was glad to turn over the lead to the older man. They had climbed only a few hundred yards farther when Blake halted suddenly. He was staring at a line of rounded tracks in the snow, cutting diagonally across their route.

"Funny," he muttered. "I wouldn't have thought anybody else was around here, weather like this. Who do you reckon wears bear-paw snowshoes?"

Skip chuckled. "I can't tell you his name," he said, "but I know his tracks all right, an' I can give you a fair description of him. He's a tall old man, stooped a little in the shoulders, with a beard an' hair that are almost white. He's quick an' strong, though, an' I'd call him a first-class woodsman. Remember, back in the fall, I asked you about a stranger on the mountain?"

"Sure," Blake replied. "You think this is the same feller?"

"I'm pretty certain. The only time I got a look at him was the day Penny Baker sprained her ankle—that time we found the beaver dam. But Joe Lukens saw him several weeks ago, when we were over on the south side, where the deer had yarded. Guess I never told you about that. We found a yard down in the swamp, with a buck an' two does an' a black an' white cow in there with 'em."

Blake nodded. "I've seen 'em," he said. "What about the man?"

"Well, he ducked out of the thicket an' made a run for it. We followed his tracks up the mountain to a high ledge, an' there we lost 'em. He pulled a slick dodge on us, we figured afterward. Must have swung up into a tree and worked along through the branches till he came out on top of the ledge. Then, when we started a cook fire at the foot of the rock, he dumped snow down on it!"

"What is he?" Blake asked. "Some kind of practical joker?"

"Search me. All I'm sure of is that he wants to keep folks away from here. Once, I guess I told you, he sprung the camera trap I'd set in a deer path, but he didn't steal the camera or damage it. Then the day I found the bear's cave, I'd left my lunch pail on a tree down the hill. He took the food but left my ax that was standing against the tree. Of course, he does snare rabbits, an' there was that otter we let out of the trap, but I couldn't swear he set it. The track we found was quite a distance off."

The warden nodded. "I meant to tell you about that trap," he said. "I came up the stream an' found it, a day or two later. On the under side of the pan, there was a letter 'K' scratched with a nail. Only man I know that marks his traps that way is Al Krouse—your friend Dutch's father. I remember twenty years ago when we were kids, he used to trap muskrats an' foxes. But as far as I know, he's been too busy farming to fool with traps for a long time now."

Skip digested this news thoughtfully. A suspicion was beginning to form in his mind, for he recalled that Dutch Krouse had not been far away when he met Penny in the school corridor and told her about finding the otter slide. He wasn't especially fond of Dutch, but he still hoped it wasn't he who had tried to trap the animal.

"You want to follow that trail?" asked Blake.

"I'd like to," Skip told him, "but I'd rather get a picture of the bear before we do anything else."

The warden nodded and moved on up the slope. When they reached the boulders below the big ledge, Skip took over the lead once more. He scrambled up the steep bank of snow and paused at the entrance of the cave, pointing to the undisturbed surface of the fresh drift.

"He's right in there," he told Blake.

The older man indicated Skip should set the knapsack beside the entrance and take the flashlight, while he held his rifle ready. Skip stepped forward boldly till he was inside beyond the drift. Once he turned on the electric torch, the cavern looked lower and smaller than it had seemed in the dark. At the narrow opening that led to the inner cave, he stopped to set the camera. Then, with the warden close at his heels, he made the bend to the left. Again the rank animal smell assailed his nostrils.

"Phew!" he heard Blake whisper behind him. They were in the second chamber now, and there, sharply visible in the beam of the torch, lay the huge, rusty-black body of the sleeping bear. With hands that shook, Skip handed the flashlight back to the warden and focused the camera. He waited a second or two to steady himself and pressed the button. At the vivid flash, the big beast stirred a little and gave a kind of growling sigh. That was all. In a moment it was as deeply asleep as ever.

"Come on," Blake murmured. "Let's get out before we suffocate."

The sunlight was dazzling after the darkness of the cave, and air never tasted so fresh and sweet.

"Think you got your picture all right?" the warden asked.

"Can't tell till it's developed, but everything seemed to

work. I bet there aren't many animal photographers that ever get such a chance!"

"That's a fact. He's the first hibernating bear I've ever seen in twenty years in the woods. Let's go see where that snowshoe trail leads to."

They picked the tracks up at the foot of the slope, and though they appeared to be headed to the southwest, Blake decided to follow them northeastward, angling down the mountainside. This route took them farther and farther from the place where they had left the jeep, but the warden didn't seem to mind any more than Skip did. Their whole attention now was centered on finding the hide-out of the mystery man.

For a mile or more, the trail led fairly straight, following the contour of the hill and avoiding fallen trees. Then suddenly it disappeared at the edge of what appeared to be an impenetrable thicket of spruce.

"Hm," Blake muttered. "Where'd he go?"

Skip remembered how he and Joe had been fooled and looked overhead for a handy branch. But there was no tree of any size close by. He shrugged and pointed at the tangle of spruce.

"Must have wiggled through there somehow," he whispered.

The older man knelt down and pulled off his mitten to feel around in the brush. After a moment Skip heard him give a grunt of satisfaction. "By thunder!" he breathed. "This stuff is loose. I can move it!"

With careful hands he began pulling away the dense spruce boughs, and the boy could see they had been cunningly arranged to form a kind of door. He crouched behind Blake and peered through the opening. At first he could see nothing but more thick-growing spruce. Then he made out a pattern of snowshoe tracks inside the first barrier. They were visible for only a few feet before they disappeared again.

Blake stood up, panting. "No doubt about it," he breathed. "This is where the fellow lives."

With that, he went boldly through the gap, and Skip followed close behind. After two or three yards they could see where the bear-paw tracks made a sharp bend to the right, circling a small clump of fir saplings.

Blake took the safety catch off his rifle before he went on. A dozen strides brought them around the fir clump, and there, so near they could almost touch it, was a tiny cabin of chinked logs, with a bark roof and a rough stone chimney.

No smoke rose from it, and there was no sound from the little hut or the cleared space around it. Nevertheless, Blake held up a warning hand and motioned to Skip to stay where he was. Very quietly he went toward the east end of the cabin, where there might be a door.

Chapter Sixteen

While Skip waited, he took a picture of the little log house. He had a feeling that the owner, whoever he might be, was not at home, but he cocked the camera again, ready for a shot if the man appeared. After a moment Blake returned.

"He doesn't seem to be around," the warden growled. "Got a padlock on the door, too, so I couldn't get a look inside. But there's someone living here, all right. He's thrown out a mess o' bacon grease, an' I could smell stale tobacco smoke."

Skip went to look for himself, and just as he rounded the corner of the cabin, he saw a slow-moving black animal come out of the thicket. He had never seen a porcupine except in pictures, but he knew at once that this was one. Quickly he aimed his camera at the creature. It seemed to pay no attention to him but waddled forward to nose at the dark patch in the snow where the bacon grease had been thrown. There were several frames left on Skip's film, and he used all but one, taking various poses of the quill-covered animal.

Blake came to stand beside him. "You're in luck, boy," he said. "We don't often get porcupines down this way. This is the first one I've seen in a dozen years."

Reluctantly Skip closed the Retina and followed the warden out through the thicket entrance. They put the spruce boughs back in place as neatly as they could and headed westward.

"I wonder what the old man'll do now," Skip speculated.

"He's sure to notice our tracks on top of his. You figure he'll pull out an' build a new camp somewhere else?"

"Hard to say," Blake replied. "But he'd have to comb these woods for years before he found a place as well hid as that. No wonder the deer hunters never spotted it! One of 'em did report to me he'd seen smoke over this way, but he couldn't locate where it came from. Well, son, we've got a long hike back to the car. What say we get moving?"

They went a different way this time, striking west for nearly a mile till they reached a fire line running southward. The going was easy along this straight path, cleared of trees and brush. When they had followed it for half an hour, they were within sight of the road, and once they reached it, they were soon at the parked jeep.

"Tired, are you?" Blake asked.

"Just a little," Skip told him with a grin. "I guess I've never traveled so far on snowshoes before."

"Well, it was a good day's work, anyhow. I'm grateful to you for telling me about the bear. And now I know where your 'old man of the mountain' hangs out, I aim to find out more about him an' what he's up to."

"Gee," said Skip, "I'd like to know myself. Let me know, won't you, Mr. Blake?"

The trip home was uneventful except for a brief stop at Mel Hicks' store. Blake went in alone and stayed only a minute or two.

"Wanted to ask him if he'd seen the old man lately," he explained when he came out. "Sure enough the feller came in an' bought a four-pound flitch o' bacon this week. Seeing that bacon grease at the cabin made me curious."

They paused part way down the mountain to eat the sandwiches Skip had brought. It was after two o'clock when they reached the Rollins's house, and after thanking the warden, Skip hurried inside with his camera. He could hardly wait to develop his roll of film and see what he had taken.

145

As the negatives came up, he grew more and more excited. Just before suppertime Penny telephoned him.

"Did you take a picture of the bear?" she asked. "I'm dying to see your films."

"I got some good ones," he told her. "But you'd better wait till the prints are ready. I'll bring 'em over to your house right after church tomorrow."

The flash-bulb shot of the hibernating bear was as good as could be expected, considering the fact that the animal's nose and face were hidden. All that was visible was a big pile of fur, but Skip thought a blowup might bring out more detail. The porcupine pictures, taken in bright, clear daylight against a background of snow, were more satisfactory. Also he was pleased to have an unexpected addition to his collection of animals. There were seventeen now, and he hoped the beaver would still be around to give him a shot of one when the ice broke up in the spring.

But almost as important to Skip was the discovery of the hidden log cabin. He had an idea Penny would be as excited about that as he was. At twelve-thirty the next day he drove up to the Bakers' front door and was greeted there by Penny herself. Under his arm he carried a manila envelope full of the new pictures.

"Here," Penny told him. "I've cleared a place on the dining-room table where we can spread them out. Is this the picture of the bear?"

She laughed when she saw it. "That's a bear?" she asked. "I'll take your word for it, but it looks like a sack of potatoes under an old buffalo robe. Hey—what's this picture of a log house?"

Skip was somewhat miffed. "Oh," he said, "that's just a cabin we found. It happens to be where the old mountain man lives. The warden and I didn't get a look at him, but we back-tracked on his snowshoe trail an' crawled in through

146

the spruce brush to the little clearing where he'd built this shack. It's where he's been hiding out, all right. Now, here are some more shots I got while we were there."

Penny stared at the pictures. "What in the world is it?" she asked, puzzled. "Looks like a small bear, only it's got a tail—and such long, stiff-looking hair!"

Proudly he explained what it was. "Blake says porcupines are pretty rare in Hickory County," he told her. "Do you know that gives me seventeen animals for my project? When I started, I thought I'd be lucky if I got ten!"

*   *   *

Christmas Eve came, and before nightfall Skip was happy to see his uncle's sports car drive into the yard. It was a visit they had expected, for Uncle Andy rarely missed a holiday at his sister's home.

Skip had been into the woods behind their lot and cut a pretty balsam fir that afternoon, and in the evening they all trimmed it together. At midnight the job was finished. Uncle Andy went to the piano and began to play softly—old Christmas tunes like "Silent Night," "O Little Town of Bethlehem," and "We, Three Kings," while they all sang. Then, before they went to bed, gifts were brought downstairs and placed under the tree.

Opening them, the next morning, was a joyful highlight of Christmas Day. Skip, who had only a modest allowance, gave simple and inexpensive things—a magazine subscription to his father and a couple of pretty aprons to his mother. For Uncle Andy, he had worked hard to make a special scrapbook with a complete set of his animal pictures, even including the new ones of the sleeping bear and the porcupine.

His own presents were more elaborate. Among a dozen other things, he got a set of new tires for the Ford from his father, two beautiful hand-knit sweaters from his mother, and a big, handsomely illustrated book, *The Wild Animals of Eastern North America,* from Uncle Andy.

It was that last gift that kept him enthralled most of the day. He studied the excellent photographs and discussed them with his uncle. Some, he could tell from the backgrounds, were taken in zoos, and a few were pictures of stuffed animals. But there were others that taught him something about photographing animals in their wild surroundings. The night shots, using some device to trip a flash bulb, were sharper and clearer than any of his own. On the other hand, he had taken three or four daylight pictures that he knew were better than some in the book.

Most important, however, were the careful descriptions of the animals and their range and habits. He knew they would help him in writing up his findings for the 4-H project. Also he got a few tips on creatures he might add to his list.

The book, for instance, listed moles as wild animals, and in the summer they were a nuisance in half the lawns in town. Wood mice also had a place in the book. He wasn't sure he had ever seen one, but at least they gave him another possibility.

Before he left for Philadelphia, Uncle Andy took Skip aside. "I'm more pleased with the present you gave me than anything else you could have thought of," he said. "If you're willing, I'd like to show it to a fellow I know who edits an outdoor magazine. Don't forget—some day I hope to see your story in print."

"Golly!" said Skip. "I'd sure like that, but writing a story sort of scares me."

"You don't have to rush, but I'd recommend that you do some thinking about what you want to say and start putting it down on paper. Just tell how you got into the project, what kind of camera equipment you used, and then the

148

circumstances of finding each animal. When you're done, you'll probably find it makes a better article if you cut out about half of what you've written."

After he had gone, Skip began mulling over the idea. It still frightened him a little, but he found that once he started organizing his thoughts on paper, it seemed less of an ordeal. In fact, by bedtime, he almost hated to stop.

In the weeks that followed, he gave most of his spare time to working up the story. A thaw made the snow too slushy for good snowshoeing in the woods, and when a freeze followed, the hummocky ice that formed was even worse. It was early March before he had a good opportunity to return to the mountain.

A cover of light snow several inches thick had fallen on a Thursday, and by Saturday morning it was clear and cold— good weather for a snowshoe trip. Skip went alone, since Joe was tied up with chores at home, and this time he decided to explore the course of the Blacksnake once more.

He parked near the bridge, as he had done before, and followed the stream in its tortuous windings, instead of taking the shorter way along the hillside. He was in no hurry. Birds were chattering and flitting among the hemlocks and the leafless hardwood trees. There were snow buntings, juncos, a few nuthatches, and an occasional jay.

The white surfaces along the creek bank bore signs of a few small animals. Rabbits had been there, and something he thought was probably a weasel. It had left a sort of shallow channel in the snow, dotted on either side with little footprints. Later, as he plowed through one of the tangles of rhododendron stems, he caught a momentary glimpse of a gray fox darting off among the trees. He whipped the camera open but was too late to get a picture.

After a while he reached the low, marshy ground below the beaver dam. The snow covered most of it, but he could see that the stream now followed a narrow channel instead of spreading through the thickets. That must mean that the dam was still holding back the water.

Skip pushed on until the dam itself was in sight. It was ragged-looking under the canopy of snow, but he knew the furry builders cared more about efficiency than appearance. As soon as he reached the higher ground alongside the dam, he looked out across a fairly large area of snow-covered ice that was the pond. Toward its upper end, he could make out the shapes of two rounded mounds that he knew were the winter lodges of the beaver.

He tried to remember what he had read about their habits in the book he had received at Christmas. It was probable, the author had said, that wild beaver went into deep hibernation in the cold months. Whether they lived on their fat, as bears did, was a question open to some argument. When beaver houses had been broken open, trappers reported finding supplies of aspen, poplar, or some other wood with succulent bark, apparently stored there for winter eating. However, it was pointed out, no ordinary lodge could hold enough food to nourish an active beaver for more than a few weeks. And each house was occupied by from four to six animals—a whole family, in fact.

"Anyhow," Skip said to himself with a grin, "I hope you're all comfortable and healthy. I'll be back for another visit when spring comes."

He took two or three pictures of the lodges, looking like small igloos under their blanket of snow. Then he moved on past the upper end of the flooded area into unexplored country. There were more thickets here, with tangled clumps of birch and poplar along the swampy stream bed. Suddenly, right ahead of him, he heard a blue jay scream a warning, and he halted, holding his camera ready. Perhaps, he thought, the bird's raucous call was directed at himself. Then he saw a long, brown, sinuous animal moving across the snow. It looked like a weasel, the way it humped its middle, then extended its body, but he was sure it was larger and much darker in color.

Through the finder he watched a gap between the trees where he hoped the creature would reappear. For nearly half a minute he waited in vain. Then, just as he thought he had missed his chance, the animal glided into view again, and he clicked the shutter. Instantly it was gone, darting into the brush, but he thought he had a picture. He hurried ahead to the place where he had first seen it, and after a brief search he found the track. It looked very much like the one he had noticed earlier—a little broader, he thought, and deeper in the snow—but surely made by some member of the weasel family.

Skip went on for several hundred yards, with progress becoming more and more difficult. Several times his snowshoes caught on the jagged limbs of trees, hidden under the snow, and he decided to turn back before he did real damage to the webs.

All morning he had been watching, half consciously, for the rounded tracks of bear-paw snowshoes. It was almost strange not to see them, for he had become used to the presence of the old man on every trip he made into the woods. As he came to the beaver pond on the way home, he actually felt disappointed that this time he would miss the stranger.

Then, right at the spot where he had stood to take pictures of the lodges, he came on fresh oval tracks right on top of his own! He looked up quickly, and there, hardly fifty feet away, he saw the old man hurrying off toward thicker cover.

Chapter Seventeen

"Hey!" yelled Skip.

The tall, bent figure turned at the sound, and for a moment the bearded face showed clear. The boy snapped the shutter of his camera. A sort of unintelligible grunt came from the gray-clad man, and he darted off into the woods, almost at a run. Skip didn't follow him, for he knew it would be a hopeless chase. He closed the cover of the Retina and plodded on homeward, satisfied that at last he had a picture of the mysterious woodsman.

The hike back to the car was made without incident. Skip was eager to look up the animal he had seen and photographed, in his new book. If it turned out to be what he hoped it was, there would be another entry for the 4-H project as well as for his magazine article.

As soon as he had put the car away, he hurried up to his room. Opening the book to the chapter on weasels, he checked a fact he already knew—that their light brown color changed to white in winter. Then, turning a few pages, he came to what he was looking for. Pictured against a background of snow was the photograph of a mink. The head, the tail, the long, slim body and short legs matched perfectly the creature he had seen that morning. And the description clinched it. "Color," it said, "a deep, rich brown, sometimes shading to tawny on the under parts. No change of color in the winter months. Size, about 24 inches from nose to tail-tip. Natural habitat, Canada and northern New England and New York, extending south along the Appalachian Range to Pennsylvania."

He was burning to tell his news to Penny, but he wanted to develop the pictures first. There were still a few unexposed frames in the camera. He used them up on shots of blue jays and other birds around the feeder, then spent the rest of the day in the darkroom. Before bedtime he had prints of all the films and was ready to start enlarging the best ones.

The weather changed in the night, and Skip woke Sunday morning to the drumming of rain on the roof and the gurgle of water from the melting snow running down the gutters. Winter, it seemed, was about over.

He went to church with his family, then returned to the enlarging. By midafternoon he had made half a dozen blowups that he was proud of. One—the picture of the old woodsman—had been enlarged twice, so that the final print was eight inches by ten. It was big enough to bring out clearly the details of the man's face.

As soon as Sunday dinner was out of the way, Skip called Penny to make sure she was at home. Then he took his pictures and drove to her house. She was excited when he showed her the blown-up prints.

"Dad," she called, "if you've got a minute, come and look at these photographs Skip took."

Eldon Baker was a man with a lively interest in almost everything. He owned and edited the local weekly paper, the *Welbyville Clarion,* and his tousled shock of gray hair was a familiar sight as he drove around the county looking for news. Summer or winter, he was never known to wear a hat.

"What have you got this time, son?" he asked genially. "Say, that looks like a mink! Good work! There aren't many around here. And who's this fellow?"

"We don't know," Penny told him. "But he lives in the woods, up back of the mountain. Skip's seen his cabin. He acts afraid of people—must be a hermit, I guess."

"Funny," the editor mused. "I don't often forget faces, and I've seen that one somewhere—maybe in a newspaper photo. You're right, though. His eyes looked scared. How old would you say he is, Skip?"

"It's hard to tell. The white beard may not mean much, and I know he's strong and quick. He could be anywhere from fifty to seventy, I'd say. For a while, I thought he was a trapper and poacher, but I'm not so sure now."

"Well," said Mr. Baker, "if you've got a spare print, I'd like to take this picture along to the office tomorrow. Maybe it'll come to me where I've seen him before."

"Sure," Skip replied. "I can make as many as I need, so take this one."

He stayed an hour longer and talked to Penny about the article he was trying to write. She gave him a lot of encouragement.

"Don't tighten up," she advised. "Just write it the way it all happened. Sure, it'll be too long—but cutting will be easy. Dad can help on that."

He drove home through the warm rain. Most of the snow was already gone, and there was a feel of spring in the air.

*   *   *

Skip worked hard that week. Third quarter exams were coming up soon, and he wanted to get his grades up before Easter vacation. The weather stayed above freezing, the snow was gone except for a few remnants of drifts in shady places, and on March 14 the first robin was reported. Mrs. Rollins came out daily to look for signs of crocus and snowdrop blossoms on the lawn.

That Thursday night there was a 4-H meeting at the Grange Hall, and Skip was on hand with his more recent photographs. The other boys had some new lambs and pigs and calves to report, but there was more interest in his own project than in any of theirs. Only Dutch Krouse appeared unimpressed.

"What you got this time?" he grunted. "Another mouse?"

He hadn't shown any pictures since Christmas time, so the shots of the hibernating bear and the porcupine were new to the group. Skip showed the picture of the mink last of all, and it caused plenty of excitement among both the girls and the boys.

"What a wonderful stole he'd make!" said Penny wistfully, and her thought was echoed by all the feminine contingent. Dutch was the last to come up for a look.

"Hey!" he said. "It *is* a mink, sure enough. Whereabouts was it you saw him?"

There was a greedy look in his eyes that Skip didn't like.

"I guess I'd better keep that a secret," he told the stocky youngster. "You're too anxious to use those traps of yours."

Dutch couldn't conceal the startled look that came over his face. Then he recovered his self-assurance.

"Traps?" he blustered. "What are you talkin' about?"

"You remember," said Skip. "That trap you set for the otter, over on the far side of the mountain. For a while we thought it was the old fellow with the beard. But the trap had a 'K' marked on it. Did you ever get it back after Penny an' I let the otter loose?"

"Why—you—" Dutch started to sputter. Then he thought better of it and turned away with a red face.

None of the other club members had heard the exchange, for both boys had been speaking in low voices. Now Joe Lukens turned from examining the pictures to ask Skip a question.

"How many animals have you got on your list now?" he said. "Must be pretty close to twenty, isn't it?"

Skip shook his head. "Only eighteen that I've really photographed," he replied. "If I can get a shot of a beaver, that'll be one more, but I doubt if I'll make twenty. Sure would be nice to, though—it's a good round number."

"How about letting me go with you when you try for the beaver? You reckon the ice is out of the pond yet?"

"It ought to be," said Skip. "I'd be glad of your company. I figured on going some day next week. How'd Tuesday do? It'll be vacation, you know."

They agreed to make an early start the following Tuesday if the weather wasn't too bad.

Over the weekend Skip wrote some more on his magazine story. Page after page of pencil-written manuscript was piling up on his desk, and he was still only a little more than halfway through. Trying to estimate the number of words to a page, he discovered he had already written close to four thousand words. With dismay he recalled his Uncle Andy's warning that he should try to keep it down to twenty-five hundred.

On Sunday afternoon he took his sheaf of manuscript over to Penny's and asked her if she thought her father would be willing to look over what he had written.

"I'm discouraged," he said. "The thing just seems to drag out longer and longer."

Eldon Baker came out of the cluttered little den where he wrote some of his editorials. "Just thinking about you, Skip." He chuckled. "I may have a lead on that mysterious old man of yours. In a day or two, I hope to get answers to a couple of letters I sent off. What's your problem this time?"

Somewhat embarrassed, Skip explained what he had been trying to do. "Here it is," he said. "It's about three times too long, and I can't seem to make it any shorter."

For three or four minutes, the newspaperman skimmed swiftly through the handwritten sheets. Then he laid them down and smiled over his spectacles.

"You've got some good, vivid description here," he said.

156

"But it's buried in a lot of detail. Nobody wants to know what road you used to get to the woods or what the weather was like every day. Remember, the pictures tell most of the story. If I were you, I'd pretend I was just writing a caption for each photo. Take this long passage about the bear robbing the beehive, for instance." And he proceeded to blue-pencil paragraph after paragraph.

"See?" he concluded. "I've left only about a hundred words, but they give the meat of the story."

"It looks easy when you do it," said Skip. "Maybe I can use this for a pattern an' do some cutting myself. The trouble must have been that I didn't know what was worth saving. Now I can see."

He thanked the editor again and took his manuscript home. That night and the following day he learned to be ruthless with the words he had labored to set down. More important, when he started writing again, he tried to say only the essential things, keeping the story brief but colorful. Perhaps he had it in him to be a writer after all.

Monday night a cold north wind began to blow, and in the morning the ground was hard with frost. Joe Lukens called up while Skip was at breakfast.

"You still want to go up to the woods?" he asked.

"Sure," said Skip. "It'll be better footing if it's frozen. Won't be so much mud. But be sure you wear warm clothes."

An hour later he picked up his friend at the farm, and they drove to the bridge over the Blacksnake. As Skip had foreseen, the ground was hard enough for easy hiking, and there were only a few mudholes to avoid. The creek, however, was still open, except for a skim of ice along the bank. They followed the higher ground along the slope to save time, and by ten o'clock they were on the hillside above the beaver dam.

"Now," said Skip, "we've got to go mighty quiet. Don't you dare step on a dry stick, Joe."

He opened his camera, screwed on the zoom lens, checked the light meter, and set the focus for a hundred feet. Approaching from the south, as he was, the sun would be behind him. If there were beaver in the pond at all, he ought to get a picture.

They were fairly close before Skip caught a glint of water through the trees. He motioned to Joe to move even more cautiously and went on, one step at a time. So far, he was sure they hadn't made any noise. Then, when they were only thirty yards from the edge of the pond, a sound broke the stillness. It wasn't made by either of the boys, and they stood openmouthed, listening.

It was a steady, muffled sound—*crunch, crunch, crunch*— and it seemed to be coming from down close to the water. Skip gripped Joe's arm in excitement. "Beaver!"—he whispered. "He's gnawing a tree!"

Crouching low, he crept steadily nearer. The brush beside the pond was thick, but at last he made out the shape of a fairly large brownish animal at the foot of a poplar sapling. The beaver was so busy cutting the trunk with its big, chisellike teeth that it was still unaware of any danger.

By lying flat on the ground, Skip found he had an unobstructed view between the bushes. He aimed the camera, steadied it across his forearm, and snapped the shutter. Apparently the animal was too much occupied with its gnawing to hear the click. The trunk of the four-inch poplar was nearly severed now, and the beaver reared back on its hindquarters and gave a push to the tree with its forepaws. With a crackle of tearing fibers, the sapling toppled over toward the pond.

Skip had his second picture and was ready for a third, but just as he stood up, the animal must have heard him or

caught his scent. Like a flash, it scuttled for the water and dove in head first.

"Quick!" Skip breathed. "I want to catch him when he comes up."

Together they went crashing through the brush to the bank. The ripples made by the beaver's plunge were fading out, and there was no sign of its reappearance. For twenty seconds or more they waited. Then, far up toward the rounded lodges, a dark head came into view. Just as Skip got it in the finder, the swimming beaver raised its broad, flat tail and struck the water with a loud slap—a warning to the rest of the colony. Immediately it dove again.

"Whew!" Skip sighed. "That was close, but I'm sure I got the shot. Let's not scare 'em any more. I want some pictures of the tree he cut down."

Joe hated to leave the spot, but he followed Skip reluctantly. For ten minutes they examined the neatly felled poplar and photographed it from various angles. There were no more sounds from the pond as long as they stayed in the vicinity. The beavers, it appeared, had taken refuge in their houses.

"Hey!" said Joe finally. "It's still early. Why don't we go up the mountain a ways? I'd like to see those caves in the rocks where you found the bear asleep."

"It's a pretty long distance," Skip told him doubtfully. "An' I've never been there from this side."

"Shucks, we can't get lost," Joe replied. "I'll blaze trees as we go, so we can find our way back. See? I've got my jack-knife."

"All right," said Skip. "I'm game to try it. Don't start complaining if it's further'n you expect, though."

They scrambled upward through tangled thickets and briars till they were on the mountainside. There the brush thinned out somewhat, but the climbing was steeper. Fallen trees and rocky outcrops made their progress slow.

After an hour Skip paused to rest. "I reckon we've come more'n halfway," he said. "The ledges ought to be right up yonder, a mile or so from here. I was just wondering how you'd feel if we ran into that hungry old bear. It's been warm the last week or so, an' he may have decided winter was over."

"Huh!" Joe snorted. "You can't scare me! Why, he'd prob'ly turn 'round an' run if he saw us."

Skip wasn't too certain himself, but he said no more. They panted on up the rugged slope till at last the sheer gray wall of the ledge loomed above them. There was no sun, and the north wind had a bite in it. But it wasn't the wind that sent a shiver down Skip's back. Looking up at the naked crag gave him a feeling that something menacing awaited them there.

Chapter Eighteen

Cautiously they climbed up among the boulders that lay at the foot of the ledge. Patches of snow were still visible in the sheltered places below the caves, and Skip studied the white surface for signs of tracks. If the bear had indeed come out, he must have left a few footprints. But there were no tracks to be seen.

Joe noticed the same thing. "Gee," he said, "he must be still in there! Let's go take a look at him."

"Not a chance!" Skip replied firmly. "Even if he's asleep, we'd probably wake him up, an' I'm not about to face a hungry bear in that little cave!"

Joe grumbled that he never had any of the fun, but he finally agreed to leave the cave alone. As they turned away, however, he noticed some cracks and narrow shelves on the face of the cliff above them. "Look!" he pointed. "I bet we could climb up there—or part way anyhow."

"It's a crazy idea," Skip told him, "but it's your neck. Go ahead if you want. Me—I'm not going to risk busting up my camera. When you get up there, I'll take your picture, so you'll be able to prove you did it."

He leaned back against a boulder and made himself comfortable while the other boy prepared to climb. Actually, Skip half expected Joe to give up the project, but his pride must have been touched. He mounted slowly, searching for handholds and crannies where his toes could find a grip. After three or four minutes, he had climbed about fifteen feet—more than halfway to the top. Skip watched with admiration but didn't speak. He was afraid Joe might lose his hold if anything disturbed him.

Doggedly Joe inched upward. Skip aimed the camera and was about to take a picture when a strange sound drifted down to him. It was a kind of coughing grunt and seemed to come from the crest of the cliff. He backed off a step or two and looked up at the rocky summit. And there, silhouetted against the dark of the spruces, was a big, tawny shape.

Skip's heart was in his mouth, for he knew he was looking into the snarling face of a full-grown mountain lion!

The cough came again, and Joe turned his head. "Hey," he called down, "what's makin' that noise?"

"Don't move," Skip told him quietly. "Just hang on tight where you are. There's some kind of animal up there."

With hands that shook a little, he pointed the zoom lens at the huge cat. Through the finder he could see the tip of the long tail twitching angrily. He clicked the shutter.

"Well," called Joe, "what sort of animal? You took a picture, didn't you?"

"It's—it's all right, Joe," Skip answered, trying to keep the fright out of his voice. "I reckon it's gone off now. You'd better start down, slow an' easy."

The cougar was still there on the top of the cliff, but the sound of their voices seemed to have given it some doubts. The tail no longer twitched. As Joe started down, his foot dislodged a stone, sending it crashing among the boulders below. And at that noise, the great cat turned silently and disappeared.

"Are you O.K., Joe?" Skip asked. "Take it slow, now. I'll get a shot of you coming down."

Once more he clicked the shutter, careful to hold the camera high enough so that the rocks at the foot of the ledge wouldn't show. In a moment the other boy jumped down and came toward him.

163

"What was it up there?" Joe asked. "A deer or somethin'?"

Skip let out a sigh of relief. "No," he said, "it was the biggest, nastiest-looking mountain lion I ever hope to see. He acted as if he was ready to jump down on you—switching his tail an' snarling. Gosh—those teeth! I figured he wouldn't see you if you stuck close to the face of the ledge. Maybe it was lucky you loosened that rock, because he left when he heard it."

Joe's eyes bugged out as he listened. "Golly!" he breathed. "I'd like to have seen him, but if I had, I'd prob'ly have fallen right off. Was it a sure-'nough mountain lion?"

"I'll let you judge for yourself when you see the picture," Skip told him. "Counting the tail, he must ha' been eight or nine feet long. An' I was looking right into those mean yellow eyes an' that mouth full of long white teeth! Come on— let's make tracks out of here before he decides to come back."

It was a long distance from the ledge on the north side of the mountain to the bridge over Blacksnake Creek, and the first part of the way they had to follow Joe's knife marks on the trees. So, by the time they reached the car, it was well along in the afternoon. Several times during the journey, Skip had had a feeling of being watched and looked back over his shoulder. Twice he could have sworn he saw a graybrown shape slinking through the brush behind him. But he said nothing to Joe, who was busy up ahead, hunting for blazed trees. Then, when he got behind the wheel to drive home, it seemed too ridiculous to mention. That first sight of the big cat must have worked on his imagination, he decided.

"Hey!" Joe whispered. "Look back up there on the hill!"

At the edge of the woods, Skip's eye caught a flash of tawny brown, then the flick of a long black-tipped tail. One instant the beast was there. In the next it was gone.

"Followin' us!" gasped Joe. "I got a good look at him, an' he's a mountain lion, all right."

Both boys were shaken by their experience. Skip drove to the Lukens' farm, and as soon as they went inside, Joe tried to telephone the game warden. It was Mrs. Blake who answered.

"I'm sorry," she said, "but Tom's up in the woods on one of his regular two-day inspection trips. I don't expect him home till late tonight."

Joe hesitated. "All right," he said at last, "I'll call him tomorrow."

"Didn't want to tell her," he explained to Skip. "Might have scared her half to death."

Skip had to agree, but he knew it was vital to get word to the warden before the huge cat killed any farm stock. After he got home, he phoned Mrs. Blake himself and told her he would wait up until her husband called him.

"Is it that important?" She laughed.

" 'Fraid it is, Mrs. Blake," he said. "I reckon Mr. Blake would want to know just as quick as possible."

It was nearly midnight when the telephone rang, and Mr. and Mrs. Rollins were long since in bed. Skip answered and was relieved to hear the warden's deep-voiced drawl.

"What's all the big mystery, Skip?" he asked. "You an' Joe in some kind of trouble?"

"He and I were up on the north side of the mountain today," Skip replied. "At the top of that high ledge above the caves, we saw a mountain lion! I got a good picture of him. But after that, he followed us all the way back to the road. Sure scared us, the way he stayed right on our trail."

"Well, doggone!" Blake ejaculated. "I figgered there was some kind of big cat around. Found a fresh-killed yearling doe over south of the mountain yesterday. You boys were probably safe enough, though. They won't attack humans unless they're wounded or cornered. An' following your trail wasn't so strange. A cougar's got more natural curiosity than any other critter. I reckon I'll have to get him in a hurry, though, or he'll be killing the farmers' sheep an' cattle. I'll round up some good dogs an' go up there after him tomorrow."

Skip was longing to ask if he could come, too, but he thought he knew what the answer would be. He had spent a good part of the evening in the darkroom and had good prints of the snapshots he had taken. He planned to set about making enlargements of two of the beaver pictures and the one of the mountain lion in the morning. The luck he had had with the last one was amazing. Every detail of the giant cat stood out clear and plain. The white ear linings and the white patches over the eyes and around the snarling black muzzle were as sharply defined as the bared teeth. Nothing was lost, even to the angry-looking black tail-tip.

He read over the chapter on the cougar in his wild animal book and was proud to realize that he had an even better photograph than the one used as an illustration. The description interested him, too. The largest of North American cats, he discovered, was rare in most areas except the Rocky Mountains and the Southwest. But it was occasionally encountered in the Appalachian region and as far south as Florida. It went by a number of different local names—cougar, puma, catamount, panther (or "painter"), mountain lion being the most common. Its principal prey was deer, but it often killed sheep, calves, and other domestic animals. A hungry cougar had been known to attack children, and on a few occasions even grown men and women. It frequently frightened human beings by following them through the woods. The only explanation given for this action was the beast's curiosity.

Skip was at breakfast the next morning when a horn honked outside. Going to the door, he saw the game warden's old station wagon in the driveway.

"Get your things on!" Blake called to him. "We need you to show us where to start the dogs."

Hardly believing his luck, Skip pulled on his boots and mackinaw. Then he grabbed the camera and hurried out to the car. Bill Hunt sat in the right-hand seat. In the back were three dogs—the rough-coated old coon-dog Rowser, a black and white foxhound, and a powerfully built bull mastiff.

As soon as Skip was in, the warden pulled out of the drive. "Tell us the last place you sighted the cat yesterday," he said. "We'll start there."

Skip gave directions, and they drove north on the Creek Road. At the bridge he pointed up across the pasture. "Right there at the edge of the woods," he said.

They parked and took the dogs up the hill on leash. Both Blake and Hunt carried high-powered rifles. When they reached the fringe of trees, old Rowser and the foxhound were turned loose to search for a scent.

"Ought to be fair trackin' weather," Bill Hunt remarked. "It's damp enough so the scent'll lie. Look—the young hound's got something!"

The black and white dog was trembling with excitement, and now he cut loose with a yelping bay. Rowser hurried to his side, nosed the ground, and gave tongue in turn. At once, they took a line uphill through the woods, while the men followed as fast as they could.

"Won't all that noise scare the lion?" Skip panted.

"Sure. That's what we want," Blake told him. "A cat won't travel many miles. He'll try an' find a good tree or a high place in the rocks."

It seemed to Skip, however, that the animal had gone a considerable distance. At the pace they were moving, he was beginning to get out of breath, and the trail led on and on, straight toward the cliff above the caves.

A dismaying thought came to Skip. Perhaps they were merely following the old trail made by the catamount when it had come down behind Joe and himself the day before. The two hounds, on the other hand, seemed to find the scent as fresh as ever, and even the mastiff pulled eagerly on his leash.

Rowser and the younger dog were out of sight, a quarter of a mile ahead, when their baying suddenly changed to a chorus of sharp, excited barks.

"Got him treed!" Bill Hunt cried.

The men with the rifles broke into a trot, and Skip kept up with them, getting the camera ready as he ran. He could tell now that the place where the dogs were barking was off to the left of the high ledge. Tom Blake looked upward, shielding his eyes, then pointed.

"Up in that big hemlock," he called. "Stretched out on a limb—see him?"

Skip caught a glimpse of the tawny body then. It was a good twenty feet above the excited hounds, glaring down at them with the fierce yellow eyes he remembered so well.

"Hold your fire, Bill," Blake said in a voice of authority. "It's my job. If I miss, you take a shot."

He released the mastiff, lifted his 30-30, and took careful aim, and at the same moment Skip clicked the camera shutter. Just as the warden fired, the big cat shifted position, moving a few inches along the limb. Then, with the crack of the rifle, there came a snarling shriek, and it launched itself downward into the midst of the dogs.

Skip was shaking with excitement, but he managed to reset the camera, focus it on the whirling melee, and snap a picture. Hunt's rifle barked then. The young foxhound had pulled clear, yapping in pain, but Rowser and the mastiff had their teeth in the catamount's flanks. Now Blake ran in, aimed from the hip, and put his second shot into the huge cat's head. Even after it lay twitching in its death agony, the dogs hung grimly on. Bill Hunt had to pry their jaws open with the hilt of his hunting knife to make them let go.

"They all got clawed up pretty bad," the warden panted, "but I reckon they'll survive."

He whistled for the foxhound, and the poor beast came, cringing, to him, its sides dripping blood from four deep slashes. From a pocket of his hunting coat, Blake took a jar of ointment and began smearing the stuff on the wounds.

"Go ahead, Bill," he told Hunt. "You begin skinning the critter out. I'll look after the dogs. How about it, Skip? Did you get any pictures?"

"I—I guess so," the boy told him. "I was scared and rattled, but I did snap one right before he jumped an' another after the dogs tackled him."

Chapter Nineteen

It was a long hike back to the car. Bill Hunt proudly carried the cougar's skin, while the warden bore the young foxhound in his arms. The other two dogs limped after them, and Skip brought up the tail of the procession.

Before they left the spot where the kill was made, he had gone over for a look at the bear's cave, not far away. The snow in front of the opening was nearly gone, but he saw something that he thought might be a bear track. There was no time to make certain, for Tom Blake wanted to get the injured dogs back to a veterinarian.

They rode in triumph down the main street of the town. Whenever Hunt saw someone he knew, he held up the cougar's grinning head and shouted out the news. So it was that by the time they reached the vet's office, the word had spread far and wide.

On his way home, Skip stopped a moment at the drugstore to tell his father what had happened, but John Rollins had already heard.

"You mean"—he laughed—"that you didn't get clawed? From the way folks have been telling it, I expected to see you dripping blood from half a dozen wounds!"

"I didn't get close enough till the lion was dead," Skip replied. "Nobody got hurt but the dogs—an' the cat himself, of course. But golly, Dad, he sure is a big one! Bill Hunt's got the skin, an' I guess he plans to have it stuffed."

"Good! I'll have to go look at it, along with the rest of the town. You know the *Clarion* ought to have this story. Why don't you go see Mr. Baker an' give him the real facts?"

Skip hurried home, got the negative of his first lion picture, as well as the small print, and went at once to the newspaper office. Eldon Baker was in the back room, busy at his desk. He pushed the green eyeshade back off his forehead and rose to welcome the boy.

"I heard a rumor about some excitement." He chuckled. "Tried to call Tom Blake to verify it, but he wasn't home yet. What happened, son?"

Skip told his story, answering an occasional question shot at him by the editor. "By now," he concluded, "I reckon Bill Hunt's put a tape measure on the hide. We figured the cat was around eight feet long, nose to tail. Here's a picture of him, if you can use it."

"Good!" Baker exclaimed. "A first-rate picture, and we'll blow it up from the negative. I wouldn't be surprised if we made the wire services with this yarn. I'll put in a call to The Associated Press, soon as I've talked to Bill Hunt."

Skip was starting to leave when the editor called him back. "I forgot to tell you, Skip," he said. "Maybe I've found out who your old man of the mountain is. About four years ago, one of the down-state papers carried a story about a college professor who got arrested for interfering with some hunters. They'd shot a deer an' wounded it. When they followed the blood trail, they found this angry old man standing over the deer and trying to keep 'em from touching it.

"The local justice of the peace decided he was crazy an' had him committed to a state hospital for observation. Well, they couldn't find much wrong with him except that he hated to see things killed. Felt he had a mission in life to protect all wild animals. He was released about a year ago. Here's his picture, the way he looked when he was arrested. Look familiar?"

Skip's heart beat faster as he stared at the blurred newspaper reproduction. The man shown was rather neatly dressed, and his beard was trimmed, but there was no mistaking the wild look in the eyes. Under the picture was a caption: "Dr. Jared Rickson, eccentric animal lover."

"It's the man," Skip said. "There can't be any question about it. I guess this explains a lot about the way he's acted, an' if I ever get near enough to talk to him, I'll apologize for things I've said about him."

For some time, the mountain lion was the main topic of conversation in Welbyville, and Skip and Joe had to tell about finding it over and over to curious boys and grownups. An enterprising reporter from New York arrived by plane as soon as the story hit the wires. He photographed the wounded dogs, the cougar skin, and Bill Hunt, posing with rifle in hand. Then he offered Skip fifty dollars for prints of his two pictures of the live animal. He accepted in a daze.

*   *   *

It was two full days before the excitement died down and Skip could go back to working on his magazine article. He wasn't satisfied with it yet, but he began to grow restless after hours at the desk. What he wanted to do was go back up the mountain and see if he had been right about the bear track. He called Joe, only to find the farm boy had too many chores to do. And Penny was away, visiting friends in Stroudsburg. So he took his freshly loaded camera and set off alone in the old car.

The air was soft and balmy as he drove around to the west side of Big Hickory and parked on the woods road above Mel Hicks' store. That, as he had found, was the shortest way up to the caves in the cliff. He climbed steadily, listening to the raucous screams of blue jays and the chirring of squirrels. It was good to be alive on a spring day like this, he thought.

Deciding he should be prepared for shots of any wildlife

173

he might see, he checked the light meter and left the camera open, dangling from its strap around his neck. Looking up the mountainside, he could see the gray face of the cliff far above. The caves themselves were still hidden by the trees.

As he started climbing once more, he caught a glimpse of movement at the edge of a thicket, off to the left. A small brown ball of fluffy fur came tumbling out into the open, and he rubbed his eyes as he realized he was looking at a bear cub.

Hastily he swung the camera up and put his eye to the viewfinder. The little roly-poly fellow saw him, sat back on its haunches, and stared, its round ears pricked up, a comical expression of wonder on its face. As Skip clicked the shutter, the cub let out a squeal and scurried back into the brush.

"Golly!" Skip breathed exultantly. "That ought to be a honey of a shot!"

He waited, hoping for another glimpse, but at that moment a big black shape came plowing out of the woods. The mother bear, alerted by her offspring's squeal, was charging down the hill like a locomotive.

Scared half out of his boots, Skip turned and ran. Just below him he saw a slim birch sapling, and with frantic haste he scrambled up the trunk into the branches. There he clung, eight or ten feet above the ground, while the tree swayed under his weight. The she-bear growled angrily and rose on her hind legs, reaching up to strike at his legs with a massive paw. He pulled his feet up as high as he could and hung on, trying to pray.

Perhaps the birch tree had been a lucky choice. It was too small in circumference for the big animal to climb and too frail to support her four-hundred-pound weight. On the other hand, it rocked back and forth frighteningly at each blow of her paw. Skip was in desperate fear that he would be shaken loose.

He had no way of telling how long he hung there, but it

seemed like hours. He could feel the strength in his arms ebbing, and he knew he couldn't last much longer. Then he heard a cracked old voice calling to him.

"Keep your hold, boy!" it cried. "Keep your hold! I'll try to get her away."

He saw a tattered gray coat and a pair of scarecrow arms brandishing a club as big as a stick of cordwood. Then he caught sight of a wild white beard blowing in the wind. The "old man of the mountain" had come to his rescue!

For a moment the bear turned away from the tree and faced this new menace. Then the cub squealed again, some distance up the hill, and with a deep-voiced grunt, the mother dropped on all fours and ambled off in that direction.

The bearded man pulled off his old slouch hat and wiped his forehead with his sleeve. "Whew!" he said. "I guess it's safe to come down now. You're lucky you reached that tree before she caught up with you!"

Skip unbent his stiff fingers and let himself slide to the ground. When he tried to speak, his voice was a hoarse croak. "I reckon it was luckier yet," he managed to say, "that you got here when you did. I've never been so scared in my life."

The old man chuckled. "I've been watching you," he said, "ever since you got out of your car. I knew the old bear had come out of the cave with her cub, and it seemed probable you might get involved with them. If you're all right now, let's go down to my cabin."

Skip closed the leather flap of the Retina, after making sure it hadn't been injured in his scramble up the birch trunk.

"You think quite a lot of that camera, don't you?" his companion commented. "At first, I was afraid you were here to harm my animal friends, and I tried to drive you off. But after months of watching you, I've found out that all you're after is pictures."

Skip explained his 4-H Club project as they walked along. "My name's Skip Rollins," he said. "Is it all right if I ask yours?"

"Perfectly all right. I'm Jared Rickson—used to be known as Dr. Rickson when I was teaching biology. This shack of mine isn't very fancy, but I try to keep it clean. You've been down here once, I believe, with the game warden. Probably saw my neighbor the porcupine. He's harmless, and we get along pretty well together. By the way, does anybody else know about the beaver colony?"

"Only the 4-H boys and girls," Skip replied. "And we've all made a promise to keep it a secret. We're almost as interested in protecting wildlife as you are, Dr. Rickson."

The old fellow shook his head. "Not quite all of you, I'm afraid. There's one boy who sets traps for otter and rabbits."

"You mean," said Skip in surprise, "it wasn't you who set that rabbit snare—the time we saw the bobcat?"

"No indeed. That was the young man I'm speaking of. I was very glad when you freed the otter—you and the girl who was with you. He's recovered, by the way. I saw him yesterday. Do you want to tell me about the cougar?"

"I guess you know most of it," Skip answered. "Perhaps you were watching. Joe and I had to tell the warden about seeing him, or he might have killed a lot of animals besides deer. Shooting him was the warden's job. I guess you weren't very happy about having him killed, were you?"

"Not happy, no. But I realize it had to be done. After I found a doe he'd killed, I couldn't feel very sorry for him, even though he plays an honest part in keeping Nature's balance."

They had reached the cabin in the thicket now. Rickson pushed open the door and invited Skip inside.

"I don't have any coffee to offer you," he said with a smile. "But there's good sweet water from the spring if you're thirsty."

176

He rinsed a metal cup and dipped it in the water bucket. Skip drank gratefully, for the adventure with the bear and his long hike had made his mouth dry. When he had finished, he grinned at the old man.

"I feel as if I'd known you a long time," he said. "You must have a pretty good line on me, too. Every time I came up here, you couldn't have been far away."

"Maybe not every time." Dr. Rickson chuckled. "But I try to keep an eye on all that goes on around the mountain. Deer-hunting season is my worst time. When I hear those guns banging, I just stay in here and feel miserable."

Once more Skip tried to express his gratitude, but the old professor shrugged it off. "I've been rewarded enough," he said, "by finding another person who feels as I do about wild things. Come back any time. Only be a bit careful about she-bears with cubs!"

It was late afternoon before Skip reached home. He told his parents about Dr. Rickson that night at supper, making something of a joke out of his adventure with the mother bear.

"The old man may be a little bit cracked," he concluded, "but I like him just the same. He doesn't hurt anybody, and he sure cares a lot about the animals up there in the woods."

His mother nodded. "He sounds like a very nice kind of man. Why don't we have him down here for a meal? Poor fellow—I doubt if he's getting enough to eat, living the way he does."

"I'll be glad to ask him," Skip told her. "Maybe he won't want to come, but I bet it would do him good."

That evening he wrapped up his typewritten manuscript and took it over to the Bakers' house. Penny was still away, but her father was at home and welcomed him. First of all, Skip told him about his lucky meeting with Dr. Rickson and how much he liked the old man. Then he got down to the point of his call.

"I hate to bother you again, Mr. Baker," he began, "but I've got the magazine article done, and it's still about five hundred words over the right length. Could you give me some help cutting it?"

"Well," the editor told him, "I happen to have a little free time. Come on in my den and let's have a look."

He read the manuscript through once, then sat there with his blue pencil poised. "What I told you must have sunk in," he said with a grin. "There aren't many wasted words here. In fact, if you want my advice, I'd send it in just as it is. Editorial rules aren't so strict that they won't print a good article just because it's long. With these pictures of yours they ought to like it."

"Gee!" said Skip in relief. "I've been sweating over it so long, I can hardly believe it's finished. I'll mail it to Uncle Andy tomorrow."

Chapter Twenty

The next meeting of the 4-H Club was held on a Friday night, and practically all the boys and girls turned out for it. Penny, home from her trip, gave Skip a big smile.

"I hear there's been lots of excitement while I was away," she said. "Are you going to tell us all about it?"

"Maybe not everybody." He laughed. "But I'll tell you, if you let me come around to see you."

Cale Douglas, the County Agent, was there that night, and the members all tried to impress him when they gave their project reports. Actually not much had happened except the birth of a few more lambs and calves. Late winter and early spring, however, were a good time for planning ahead, and the young people described what they hoped to do in the coming season.

When it was Skip's turn, he set up the screen and projector, then turned to face the audience. "You all know what my project was. I wanted to find out how many different wild animals there are here in Hickory County an' prove it with photographs. I reckon I'm about finished now. There may be one or two I've missed, but these last few weeks I've been extra lucky. The total's up to twenty now—all the way from field mice to mountain lions. Everybody in Welbyville knows by now that a full-grown catamount was killed by Tom Blake an' Bill Hunt, up on Big Hickory. It was two 4-H members that saw him first, though—Joe Lukens and I. Here's the picture I got that day."

When the lights were turned off, he slipped the slide into the projector, and the great, snarling cat was there on the screen, as big and fierce as life. A chorus of surprised screams came from the girls, along with muttered "Wows!" and "Gollies!" from the boys.

"We also took pictures of a beaver that day," Skip went on, "and here they are. You've seen all the rest, but these two are the nineteenth and twentieth animals on my list. The cat, of course, is the one I'm proudest to have. I've filled out all the pages in the Wildlife Project Number Four form, too, and our club leader's signed 'em."

He turned off the projector light and sat down. In the momentary darkness, a guttural voice spoke from the back of the room.

"Twenty, huh? Well, there's one more varmint up there in the woods that somebody oughta shoot. It's that crazy old coot with the beard. He's liable to hurt somebody if he ain't rode out of the county on a rail."

Then the lights came on again, and Skip stood up, his face pale with anger.

"Dutch," he said, "I guess it's time I told you a few things. That old man you call a 'varmint' is a college professor, with a doctor's degree. The only thing wrong with him is that he's fond of all wild animals an' wants to keep 'em from being killed. I know why you hate him. Those traps an' snares he's sprung were yours—set out of season an' against the law. Don't try to deny it. There was a letter 'K' on the trap I opened to let the otter go. Well, this Dr. Rickson is a friend of mine an' I like him. I've got good reason to. He saved my life the other day!"

All the faces in the room were turned toward Dutch Krouse now, waiting for what he had to say. He sputtered something unintelligible, then got up and tramped out of the meeting, his scowl like a thundercloud. His departure eased the tension. Half a dozen excited voices were asking questions.

"Is that right about saving your life? . . . What happened? . . . Have you really met him an' talked to him? . . . Does the warden know what Dutch has been doing?"

Ed Jones, the club leader, whispered something to the County Agent, then rapped for order.

"Hold it!" he commanded. "You'll all be able to talk to Skip later. Right now we have to decide what should be done about Dutch Krouse. I don't like to suggest any disciplinary action until he's had a chance to defend himself, but he walked out with nothing to say. If there's proof he's been breaking the law, we'll have to take it up with Mr. Blake, the game warden. And meanwhile, I'm afraid Dutch should be suspended from membership. Anyone want to make that a motion?"

It was so moved and carried. The only dissenting vote was Skip's, for now that he had cooled off, he was sorry he had brought Dutch's misdeeds into the open. However, as soon as the meeting broke up, he was too busy answering questions to think much about it.

When he drove Penny home, she was serious and troubled. "I feel bad," she said, "that I misjudged the old mystery man. I was just scared, I guess, and so was he—scared that somebody'd find him out and arrest him again. Now that I know more about him, I'd like to meet him and apologize to him. Did he really save you from the bear, Skip? Do you think she'd have knocked you out of the tree?"

"I was so tired she could have, easy enough. Thank goodness I didn't have to find out, because while Dr. Rickson was standing up to her with his club, she heard her baby squalling and went away. Tell me, Penny, was I too rough on Dutch?"

"I think you did right. He's always had a mean streak in him, and I don't wonder you got mad at what he called the old man. Seems to me it was fairer to accuse him to his face than to say it behind his back."

Her words made him feel better, for he knew Penny was too honest not to tell him if she had thought him wrong.

"O.K.," he said. "I won't worry about it, then. There's just one thing—Dutch is so sore right now, he might do something foolish to get even. I sort of wish we'd had a real fight. He'd probably have licked me, but it might have cleared the air."

*　　*　　*

On Saturday there was a long distance call for Skip from his uncle. The manuscript and photographs had been delivered to his friend, the magazine editor, and he was pretty certain they would be published.

"That's not all," said Uncle Andy. "He wants to use your color shot of the hawk and the weasel for the cover of that issue!"

Skip nearly dropped the phone in his excitement, but the older man was still talking. "I hope," he went on, "that you won't stop with this first article. There ought to be more wildlife conservation stories you can illustrate, now that you've broken the ice. Next time you come down to see me, I'll take you around and introduce you to the editor. He'll have some suggestions for future articles, I expect."

Skip thanked his uncle and promised to come to Philadelphia as soon as school was out in June. After he hung up, he had to pinch himself to be sure he wasn't dreaming. A successful magazine writer at his age! Then he grinned.

"Careful, boy!" he told himself. "Better not start getting a swelled head!"

He managed to wait till Sunday afternoon before telling Penny his big news. Her excitement was as great as his own, and they were celebrating with bottles of Coke when the Bakers' doorbell rang. Penny went to answer it. A moment later she was back, her forehead wrinkled with lines of worry.

"Skip," she said, "there's a man here wearing a deputy sheriff's badge. He wants to talk to you, and he wouldn't tell me what it's about."

The face of the young man standing on the steps was grim, and the holstered revolver at his hip had an ominous look.

"Your name Rollins?" he asked. "I'm supposed to bring you down to Doc Atchison's office. There's somebody there the sheriff wants you to identify. I'll take you in the county car."

Dr. Atchison was not only a practicing physician but also the coroner, and the thought of what he might find there made Skip shiver.

"Is—is it an old man?" he asked, as they drove down the street.

"Yep," said the deputy. "He ain't dead, if that's what you're wonderin'. Just hurt pretty bad."

They found several men gathered in the doctor's office. Tom Blake, the warden, was there, along with the sheriff, the coroner, and a gaunt, bearded figure stretched out on the operating table. It was this man who spoke first, as he turned his head and caught sight of Skip.

"Hi, sonny," he said weakly. "These people don't seem to know me. Will you tell 'em who I am?"

"Sure, Dr. Rickson," said Skip. "What happened to your leg?"

"He's got a .22 rifle slug in it," said Blake. "I found him up by the beaver dam this afternoon. He says he was shot last night an' couldn't get back to his cabin."

"You know him, Rollins?" the sheriff interrupted. "Think there's any chance he might have shot himself?"

Skip shook his head. "No—he wouldn't own a gun. Dr. Rickson spends all his time trying to protect animals from hunters an' trappers."

Dr. Atchison finished bandaging the wounded leg. "Maybe you can find out who shot him," he told Skip. "He couldn't tell us—or wouldn't."

Skip bent above the patient, looking into the drawn face. "Can you talk?" he asked gently.

"The one that set the traps," murmured the old man. "He was shooting at my beaver." The weak voice faded to a whisper, and he appeared to lose consciousness.

Tom Blake nodded. "That's good enough for me," he said. "It was young Dutch Krouse. He's been doing some illegal trapping I know of, an' when the old fellow tried to keep him from killing beaver, Dutch let fly with the .22. When you pick him up, sheriff, the odds are you'll find his rifle's been fired."

The sheriff was a big, slow-moving man. He stood there chewing meditatively for a moment, then sighed. "Reckon you're right," he said. "Too bad—I've known the Krouses a long time. But that Dutch is a pig-headed youngster, an' if he don't get his own way, he can be mean."

He picked up his wide-brimmed hat and put it on. "Come on," he told the deputy. "Let's get out there."

Before they reached the door, however, it was thrown open by a heavy-shouldered man Skip recognized as Al Krouse. There was a black scowl on the farmer's face, and he had a grip on the arm of his unwilling son.

"Sheriff," he growled, "I was lookin' for you. My boy's got somethin' to tell you."

He shoved Dutch forward. "Come on, *dummkopf!*" he said. "Talk up, yet!"

"I—I was shootin' my little rifle," the boy blubbered, "an' I hit a feller, accidental. He fell down, an' I come on home. Then I got scared an' told Paw. But when we went back in the woods to look for him today, he was gone—nothin' there but a spot o' blood."

The sheriff nodded unhappily. "We've got the old feller

here, shot bad in the leg. Guess I have to take you in, Dutch. If 'twas an accident, like you say, it won't go too hard on you. Otherwise, you're in real trouble. Good thing we found the man or he might ha' bled to death."

"You hear that?" Al Krouse barked, giving his son a shake. "A murderer you could be!"

At that moment a feeble voice came from the table. "No!" it cried. "No! He was shooting at a beaver. I jumped out in front of him, warning him to stop. He didn't mean to hit me. It was an accident!"

Tom Blake stepped forward then. "Maybe this is my department, too, sheriff," he said. "You can probably hold the boy on a charge of careless use of firearms. But beaver are protected in this state, so it's a serious violation of the game laws. There could be a pretty heavy fine for that."

Dr. Atchison had hurried to the side of the old woodsman. "I think there's been enough fuss here," he said. "My patient's got to have some rest. He ought to be in a hospital bed, if we had a hospital in Welbyville."

"Doc," said Skip, "we'd like to have him at our house. Let me call up my mother—I know she'll say yes."

The coroner stroked his chin, then gave a chuckle. "Go ahead," he said. "I know Mrs. Rollins is a good nurse, an' about the best cook in Hickory County. Looks to me as if this fellow could use some nice, tasty vittles while he's recovering."

Ten minutes later Skip was riding beside old Dr. Rickson in the sheriff's car. This had been quite a day, he couldn't help thinking. Now that his wound was clean and well-bandaged, the old woodsman was sure to regain his health under Mrs. Rollins's care, and Skip was selfish enough to look forward to a good long visit with him. What talks they would have about the wild things in the forest!

He felt sorry for Dutch, who would probably be working out his fine under the stern eye of his father. Still, he deserved some punishment. Perhaps the scare he had been given would change his attitude. Soon, Skip hoped, he would be welcomed back into the club and have another chance to prove he could show the best hog at the fair. Whatever mistakes a boy might make, 4-H gave him a chance to redeem himself. A great outfit, Skip thought proudly. He was glad he belonged.

www.ingramcontent.com/pod-product-compliance
Lightning Source LLC
Chambersburg PA
CBHW060601190726
48283CB00003B/1102